‘Parents divorce, but children don’t.’

Divorce has become much more common over the recent years and, at the present rate, it means that one child in five will experience a marriage break-up by the age of sixteen.

What effect does the parents’ divorce have on their children? For the first time children speak for themselves in interviews recorded for a Thames Television series. They speak with perception about the pain and confusion of their parents’ separation and the continuing conflict of loyalty and love for both parents. They also speak of their need for continued information and discussion after the divorce and, perhaps above all, the children demonstrate a generosity, humour and resilience in their adjustment to a profound change in the structure of their lives.

Voices in the Dark

Children and Divorce

Gillian McCredie and Alan Horrox

London
UNWIN PAPERBACKS
Boston Sydney

First published in Great Britain by Unwin Paperbacks 1985.

UNWIN ® PAPERBACKS
40 Museum Street, London WC1A 1LU, UK

Unwin Paperbacks
Park Lane, Hemel Hempstead, Herts HP2 4TE

George Allen & Unwin Australia Pty Ltd,
8 Napier Street, North Sydney, NSW 2060, Australia

Published by Unwin Paperbacks in association with Thames Television International, 149 Tottenham Court Road, London W1P 9LL

ISBN 0 04 649037 X

Typeset in 10 on 11pt Times by Grove Graphics, Tring, Herts,
Printed in Great Britain by
Cox and Wyman Ltd., Reading, Berks.

Contents

*Acknowledgments*

For the children whose voices are heard in this book and for their parents.

Preface

Erica De'Ath, *National Children's Bureau*

Over the last decade the divorce rate has risen dramatically in Great Britain which means increasing numbers of children experience the separation and divorce of their parents. Many of us now have first hand experience of the effects of divorce – if not in our own marriages, then through friends or relatives. The acceptance of divorce as part of life is noticeable when we realise the extent to which it regularly occurs in television serials, documentaries and dramas, providing a mixture of fact and fiction, comedy and concern, real-life drama and stereotypes. This book was written to accompany a six-part series made by Thames Television educational department and will be of interest and value to all those coming into contact with children whose parents may be going through a separation, divorce or remarriage.

For the many thousands of children experiencing the actual separation and consequences of divorce it is likely to be a continuous process of change and adjustment. There has been little research into how it feels or on how we might prepare both parents and children better for the changes in their daily family life. This book, based on personal conversations with children, presents moving accounts of their reactions to their parents break-up, the fantasies and anxieties they retain for their absent parent, the concern and responsibility they feel for the parent who stays with them, and the wealth of emotions – of depression, sadness, embarrassment, anger, guilt and loneliness – experienced during the months and years following the separation.

Parents' own lack of emotional resources often leads to an inability to provide the kind of ordinary parental support expected during a time of crisis and children are left helpless, confused and lonely. This book provides a valuable insight for all those who come into contact with young people – especially, teachers, youth workers, and GPs. The need for someone to understand their feelings, to be there to listen to them but not to pity or intrude is a recurrent theme.

Having lost one parent through divorce and adjusted to life as a single parent family most of the children express anxiety and outright resistance to any further changes – particularly remarriage. With a remarriage rate of one in three and over one million children growing up in stepfamilies we would all do well to take note of these children's views and experience.

One of the most important messages running through this book is the children's recognition of the importance of a continuing relationship with both parents. Children want to be consulted and involved in decisions that will dramatically affect their future lives. They do not want the responsibility of making the decisions but they do want their parents to respect their needs sufficiently to talk to them, to explain what is happening and discuss how they can cope with the changes in store for them. If you have any doubts about whether conciliation services should involve children this book gives ample reasons for planning to include them – not only to allow for a clear expression of what is going to happen but to reinforce the importance of the continuing parental responsibility even though a marraige may have ended.

Being a parent is not an easy task and the process of divorce has highlighted the potential conflict, which is not always recognised, between balancing the parents' own needs as adults with those of their children. Perhaps we can do no better than to turn to these conversations with children in trying to understand and meet some of their needs—listen to them when they want to talk, consult them when decisions are to be made, explain what is happening and, most important, respect their feelings, their love and concern for both parents.

Introduction

'Parents divorce, but children don't.'

In this book, children and young people tell of the experience of divorce. They speak with painful clarity about living through the process of family break-up. They describe in intimate and honest detail the struggle to understand and accept this dramatic change in their lives.

Only a generation ago, conventional wisdom viewed divorce as a failure to uphold the cherished institution of marriage. If possible, people should rather soldier on 'for the sake of the children'. Today, divorce is widely regarded as the inevitable consequence of a destructive and dying relationship, best abandoned before it does more damage to parents and children alike. Then as now, parents often justified their decisions (whether to stay together or to separate) by claiming to act in the best interests of the children. But however much the heart-searching, parents have tended to put their own interests first when deciding whether or not to divorce. In a sense, this is entirely understandable, since parents have a primary responsibility to their own survival and fulfilment. Nevertheless, as divorce has become more common, the number of children affected has increased dramatically. At the present rate, one child in five will experience a marriage break-up by the age of sixteen.

Surprisingly, until quite recently, little research was done to assess the long-term effects of divorce on children. Only in the last decade has this gap begun to be filled. A detailed review of recent work in this area has been compiled by Martin Richards of the Cambridge Child Care and Development Group. Crudely, studies of the field have divided into two basic approaches. On the one hand, some researchers have argued that the experience of divorce is more damaging to children than growing up within an unhappy marriage, while others have offered evidence to support exactly the opposite view. After the break-up, some believe that children benefit most from continuing contact with both parents, while others argue that this can be deeply unsettling.

For example, the eminent psychoanalyst Anna Freud argued (with others) in *Beyond the Best Interests of the Child* (1973) that it is preferable for custody to be allocated clearly to one parent, in practice generally the mother, while the non-custodial parent, usually the father, should be allowed access rarely and on terms to be defined by the custodial parent. The position is summarised thus:

> Children have difficulty in relating positively to, profiting from and maintaining the contact with two psychological parents who are not in positive contact with each other. Loyalty conflicts . . . may have devastating consequences by destroying the child's positive relationship to both parents. Thus we are led to conclude that in many cases it is best for the child to lose all contact with the non-custodial parent.

This view derived to some degree from the influential work of John Bowlby, published in *Attachment and Loss* (1969) which concentrated on the effects of the child's early separation from the mother. Bowlby's research identified the profound long-term effects of separation and was widely incorporated into thinking about the impact of divorce on children.

Not everyone, however, supports the conclusion of Anna Freud and others that custody after a break-up should be clearly allocated to one parent, excluding the other. A number of major studies during the last decade have contradicted this view, among them the key work, *Surviving the Break-Up* by Wallerstein and Kelly (1980). On the basis of a long and detailed study of a group of Californian children, the authors argue that a continuing relationship with both parents is of prime importance to the continuing development of the children. They write:

> Where possible, divorcing parents should be encouraged and helped to shape the post-divorce arrangements which permit and foster continuity in the children's relationships with both parents . . . Only in exceptional circumstances should there be little or no contact between the child and the non-custodial parent . . . By five years (after divorce) the factors that contributed to good outcome and to poor outcome . . . reflect primarily the quality of relationship with both parents, the quality of life within the divorced family, and the extent to

which the divorce itself provided the remedy which the adults sought. Neither the age nor the sex of the child were relevant at this time.

Wallerstein and Kelly note that children's responses to divorce vary significantly with age. For example, children in the three-to-five age range were frightened, confused and uncomprehending; in the six-to-eight age range children felt deeply rejected, were afraid to show their anger and had an intense desire for reconciliation. Between the ages of nine and eleven, children were more able to understand what had happened and to express their feelings of anger and rejection. Adolescents aged from twelve to eighteen were most openly upset by their parents' break-up. They were preoccupied with their own identitities and expressed strong feelings about their own and their parents' relationships. But whatever the age of the child, feelings of sadness, depression and anger were common responses to all break-ups.

As many researchers have noted, the general reactions experienced by most children are similar to the mourning process following a bereavement: the initial shock and denial of the loss, followed by anger at abandonment, leading in turn to a period of depression and arriving at last at a gradual acceptance and adjustment to change. However, the mourning process can follow this clearly defined path precisely because there is a finite point at which the loved one died. By contrast, in marriage break-ups the process is often messy, confused, ambiguous or contradictory. Many children literally do not know whether the parent is 'coming or going'. There may be no clear point at which the departing parent leaves the home. Moreover, he or she remains alive, absent through choice, not through death. The child has to continue to deal with the loss and separation indefinitely, as parents and children remain together but apart. In this respect, marriage break-up is different from the mourning process following a bereavement and is arguably more demanding for the children involved.

Most recent research confirms the view that a continuing relationship with both parents is profoundly helpful to the child's adjustment to divorce. In response to this conclusion, many countries have altered their legal and social machinery to help families negotiate this painful process in such a way that the child retains links with both parents. For example, in Sweden and New Zealand and in many states of the USA there is a presumption that custody will be shared jointly after divorce. Joint custody does not itself determine living arrangements and usually the child will continue to live mainly in the home of one of the parents. But it does confirm that both parents continue to have an active role in the child's upbringing. Martin Richards comments:

> With sole custody the non-custodial parent appears to be excluded. Joint custody avoids the need for disputes in which custody is 'lost' and 'won' and confirms a view that divorce does not necessarily separate parents and children . . . Indeed, it might be more in accord with the psychological evidence if courts automatically granted joint custody unless strong reasons were brought forward to show why this is inappropriate.

In England, only about 2½% of all court orders are for joint custody. But there is some recognition that the courts can do more to help. The Booth Committee, for example, recommended:

> Joint custody should be the starting point for the parents and the Court in considering the arrangements for the children . . . We think that if joint custody was the normal order, it would encourage the parties to settle their differences and would assist conciliation on such questions as access . . . The concept of joint custody with both parents sharing in all the important decisions relating to the children would seem to be a natural corollary of divorce based upon the one ground of irretrievable breakdown of marriage.

A further way to reduce conflict both during and after break-up is through conciliation. The conciliator acts as an arbitrator to help parents settle their differences and to reach agreement between themselves without recourse to an expensive and bitter legal battle. In Britain conciliation services are not widespread. There are in-court services which are paid for out of state funds and where the conciliator is usually a member of the probation services or a registrar. There are also 'out of court' services, such as the Bristol Courts Family Conciliation Scheme, which are supported by charitable funds and by legal aid payments. Researchers found that the Bristol service reduced bitterness, made separating couples more ready to honour the access and custody arrangements they had agreed, and in one out of six cases led to reconciliation. These services are only available in limited areas and are currently under threat from government cutbacks.

Other countries have a more developed system of conciliation. In the USA, for example, there are ten thousand conciliators working; twenty-five states provide such a service and four have made it mandatory for the courts to refer certain separating couples to a conciliation service. In California, where all separating couples with children have to consult a conciliator, the number of contested cases in the San Francisco courts has dropped from 2,200 to eight.

In New Zealand, the Family Courts apply a graded scheme of conciliation and mediation. Any married person can go to the court office and discuss their problems with a counsellor. If a couple then decide to separate, the husband and wife attend conciliation sessions in order to produce an agreement where both parents can maintain their relationship with the child. The Family Court judges and solicitors have a statutory duty to promote conciliation. If all else fails, a mediation conference will be held, presided over by a judge. The lawyers may be present, but they sit at the rear of the room and are only allowed to participate at the request of the judge. In any defended custody or access cases the children are separately represented by solicitors in order to ensure that the child's interests are properly expressed.

In the past, books, newspapers, films and television have often explored family break-up through the eyes of adults. In *Kramer v. Kramer* for example, the plot focuses primarily on the struggle between the parents, as the title suggests, rather than on the feelings of their child, Billy. The interviews in this book, which were carried out as research for a Thames Television series, *Voices in the Dark*, record those feelings through the words of the children themselves. It is not an academic study of the effects of divorce on children, but a first-hand account of their experiences. Forty-five boys and girls, aged between seven and nineteen, were interviewed about divorce and its aftermath. The majority were working class, living in London, mostly with their mothers, though five lived with their fathers and one with a grandmother. The interviews took place at home, usually in the child's bedroom. The child decided the length of the interview, which often lasted several hours. Parents had given their permission but were not present. Names and personal details have been changed so that the children remain anonymous.

For a number of the children, it was the first time they had discussed their parents' divorce with anyone. Perhaps for this reason they often spoke with a vividness and a directness that was very moving. There were indications that children underplayed the pain of their parents' separation. For example, though children described their sadness and distress, they generally omitted any mention of symptoms like bedwetting or sleepwalking (which were revealed in conversations with parents, brothers, and sisters). Some children had strong views about the appropriateness of what they said. For instance, while Mike, a fourteen-year-old, was speaking of his mother's men friends, he confessed, 'I would like to talk to you more about what goes on, about my mother, but it wouldn't be right.'

One theme stood out above all others in the interviews: the lack of communication between parent and child. At best, most children were told only misleading half-truths. They were given little real information or explanation either during or after the break-up. Few, if any reasons were given for the separation. Parents left home without saying where they would be staying. New boyfriends or girlfriends were introduced unconvincingly as lodgers or housekeepers. It is hardly surprising therefore, that the sequence of events as told by the children was often confused. The children had to act like detectives, watching for clues and searching for explanations. The parents were generally unable to recognise the divorce as a continuing process rather than a single event. As the children grew older, they needed new and different kinds of information. They needed further discussion and explanation of the events that had changed their lives so profoundly. Again and again, the children said that it was the failure of adults to take seriously their needs and their views that made adjusting to divorce so difficult.

When parents decide to end a marriage the children are largely powerless to influence events. The interests of parents and children may very well be different. With only one exception, all the children interviewed had wanted their parents to stay together, even in families where there had been arguments and fights over many years. Researchers such as Wallerstein and Kelly confirm that children would in most cases prefer to live in an unhappy home than experience their parents' separation. Here the children's views conflict directly with many contemporary adult assumptions about divorce.

The children, not surprisingly, found the break-up chaotic and painful. They spoke of sadness, depression and loneliness. This was especially true for only children who lacked the emotional support of brothers and sisters. The profound feelings of loss were even more difficult to bear when one parent disappeared without trace, as happened quite often. In line with much of the research mentioned earlier, the children wanted their relationships with both parents to continue in a way that was loving and stable. They felt loyalty for both parents and they resisted pressure to take the side of one parent against the other. Even so, they frequently found themselves caught up in the parents' conflicts, which continued in many cases for years after the break-up. Children resented being interrogated by one parent about the other and often this made access visits uneasy and stressful. Ideally, the children would have liked their relationship with each parent to be accepted and respected by the other. This seldom happened.

Many recent studies have shown how access visits diminish in frequency and regularity over time. Two years on from separation, less than half of children have frequent or continuous access and about one third hardly ever see their non-custodial parent. This was confirmed by a number of the children interviewed who had virtually no contact with their non-custodial parents, all of them fathers. The children explained this with various reasons: moving home, changing job, remarrying and starting a new family. But beneath these 'explanations' the children felt a deep sense of loss and grief often expressed in the form of studied indifference or straightforward anger. The children felt both rejected and abandoned.

For others, however, relationships with their fathers actually improved after separation – a sobering comment on the lack of involvement of some fathers in family life. The shock of the marriage break-up may have forced fathers to re-examine the nature and importance of their relationships with their children. In this situation, children saw their fathers for regular and enjoyable outings in a way that had seldom happened before the divorce.

Children had to cope not only with their own unhappiness but also with the sadness and depression of their parents. They were concerned and sometimes frightened by their parents' behaviour. Often children became companions to the remaining parent. They took on responsibilities for running the home and caring for younger brothers and sisters. In effect, some children became substitute partners for their parents, especially where there was an only child. Teenage boys were frequently designated the new 'man of the house' even where there was an older sister. All these added responsibilities forced children to develop a maturity beyond their years, which in turn built up their self confidence and developed their understanding of the complexity of human behaviour. But these added responsibilities were generally a burden which the children did not welcome. In particular, they did not want to bear the load of their parents' emotional distress. They wanted to be free to be children.

Children often had to adjust to new partners in their parents' lives. When the children had borne the brunt of an increased intimacy with their parents, it was doubly difficult to feel rejected in favour of someone else. The children were understandably wary of further changes and feared that the new person would take away their parent's love and attention. Moreover, remarriage marked an end to the child's hopes that its parents would get together again. Feelings of anger and hatred towards the intruder were common. Girls in particular described how they tried to frighten off their mothers' prospective partners. Resentment was even greater when the new parent tried to take the place of the 'real' but absent parent. As Martin Richards states,

> It is important that remarriage does not lead to the exclusion of the father (or mother) and that we give up the unreal and outdated notion that parents can be easily replaced by a new parent figure. The indications are that a child is more likely to accept a new partner for their custodial parent, if they had a good relationship with the non-custodial parent. There is no argument for the simplistic notion that children are only capable of relation to two adults so that the acceptance of a step-parent is dependent on the exclusion of the original one.

Given time, many children began to realise that there were gains to be had from step-parents. In some families, domestic life became better organised and more stable. Above all, the step-parent removed from the child the burden of responsibility for the emotional support of the parent.

In conclusion, the children suggested a number of ways that parents might help them adjust more easily to separation. They emphasised repeatedly the need for open and honest communication. They asked that children be consulted or at least informed about the various changes that follow a family break-up. Equally important was the plea that parents respect and support their wish to continue a real relationship with both parents. In essence, they wanted parents to recognise that 'Parents divorce, but children don't.'

Throughout the interviews, children spoke with sensitivity and perception about their own needs and those of their parents. They showed humour and resilience in the face of difficult circumstances. For those who might feel that the interviews lack maturity and objectivity and are therefore somehow invalid, we believe the children's statements are their own best defence. Researchers have often observed that adults tend to play down the effects of divorce on their children, for understandable reasons. Often there is a gulf in perceptions between parents and children when relating the same family stories. For this reason, there may be some who find the children's comments upsetting and regard them as overstated. But these interviews offer a first-hand account of the children's feelings, and serve an essential purpose.

The quotations are interspersed with a brief commentary which aims to highlight general themes that recur throughout the interviews. In some respects, these general points may seem obvious. Detailed case histories of individual children are not provided, nor do we have a professional background that would allow us to analyse such material in real depth, were we to present it. For these reasons, there is no detailed interpretation offered for each quotation. To take one example, clearly many of the themes that arise during family break-up derive from the classic oedipal conflicts. But without providing detailed accounts of each child, and without the necessary therapeutic background in our own work, it would be both intrusive and inappropriate to offer interpretations of this kind.

In one sense, we present the interviews at face value, believing they deserve attention on their own terms. Each of these children has struggled, with little help from adults, to understand their family situations and to produce their own explanations and answers. We have no wish to set aside our own responsibility for this book, but we believe its real value lies first and foremost in what the children themselves have to say, in their own words and in their own ways, about this profound upheaval in their lives.

CHAPTER ONE

Living through the break-up

> One night I was asleep and suddenly I just woke up. It was about midnight and I saw the light was on, and I heard rowing. It was my mum and dad and they were having a fight, and all I heard was glass smash, and things falling on the floor and I sat there and cried – I just cried.

The children's memories from the period of the break-up of their parents' marriages were often fragmented and confused and gave an incomplete picture of what happened. But one stood out above all others: the memory of conflict, the fights and arguments, the tears and recriminations, the bitter warfare between two parents, as Tim describes above. In some families these occurred in sharp explosions, whilst in others they were prolonged over a period of years. One girl, Marilyn, described how it was:

> They used to have such really bad arguments and you could hear them all over the house. You could hear them yelling at each other. And then they'd go through a period in which they wouldn't talk. If you went to dad, dad would say, 'Go and tell your mother so and so'; and then mum would say, 'Well you go back and tell your dad so and so.' And so we were sort of go-betweens. I hated that.

These conflicts shook the children's lives and made them feel frightened and insecure. They had little understanding of what was happening and this increased their uncertainty and anxiety. The parents themselves were also confused and disturbed, and preoccupied with their own problems. Often, they no longer had the emotional resources to provide normal parental support – and they felt unable to discuss these upheavals with the child. Terry for example, objected to this.

> When they rowed they told us to go upstairs, and then, of course, we were so scared and everything and crying. But we wanted to see what was happening and sometimes we tried to stop it. When I used to tell them to stop, they said 'Just go away' and my mum often said it was nothing to do with me. But I used to say, 'Well, it *is* to do with me'. Then she used to say 'It's got nothing to do with you, it's just *my* life', and I used to say that I was part of it.

Some children described in detail the disintegration of their parents' marriage in which one parent was increasingly absent from home. The children were alert to the changes that were taking place but often reluctant to face up to their significance. So when the break-up finally occurred, as in Pamela's case, it was unexpected.

> Dad started to stay out, working a lot, and I really thought he was working. And I remember we used to come downstairs and find mum crying and she'd say 'Oh the housework's getting on top of me', or something like that. And now I look back on it and I realise that it wasn't that, and I feel really ashamed that I didn't suss anything.

Marilyn realised more clearly than Pamela what was happening between her parents, but although she 'kind of expected it', the final break-up still came as a shock.

> They sort of drifted apart and dad used to go out at night and not come back till the next evening. He used to say 'I'm going down bingo,' and mum never thought anything of it, and then she said 'Can I come with you?' and he said 'No, I'm going on my own.' And then he started going out every night of the week, and he'd take fresh clothes with him, and mum used to stay in with us, and she'd jolly us along, and get us a bar of chocolate from the shop. We used to play records and sit and have a chat, and play games. We went through a craze of Monopoly, and we played cards. And then they used to have arguments and dad said to mum, 'Well, you're a fat cow, and that's why I never take you out.' Those were his exact words. And he said, 'I wish I'd never married you.' I mean, it's horrible to hear your dad talking to your mum, like that. I didn't like

it. I didn't like to hear that, I mean I'm not ashamed of my mum. I don't think any woman could live like that really. Then all the people started telling her, 'Oh your Pete, he's seeing somebody else, her name is Julie and she works in the bingo.' He didn't spend much time here, so you know I sort of expected it, but when it happened it was a shock.

A common fear was that the verbal violence would spill over into physical violence. Even when this did not happen in reality, the fantasy remained. When violence did occur it usually took the form of father attacking mother. The child was afraid that the violence would run out of control and that one or both parents would be seriously harmed. Terry felt helpless:

There was one scene when he came in and grabbed her and he took her upstairs into my bedroom and he was hitting her, and she was telling me to phone for the police. I didn't know the number, and I was saying 'But I don't know what their number is', and my dad was saying 'Just don't do nothing, just sit down.'

John saw that there were some limits to the violence, but the fear remained:

He was always physical, and there was always a lot of thumping, but mum hit him too and sometimes dad had to pick up a chair, so that she'd stop hitting him. It was like there was a kind of agreed maximum and he never went over it. It was like a boundary sort of thing, but I think we were all afraid that one day he would go over the boundary and that's when you really got to start worrying because things could get very nasty then.

In one family, the father attacked the mother, and the mother in turn attacked the daughter, Helen:

My father used to hit my mother in front of me, I can just remember one occasion when she was sprawled across the floor, then he led me away, I bent over to touch her shoulder and asked her if she was all right, and she was crying. And he took me into the other room. I suppose it did upset me, but it didn't upset me at the time. I remember I didn't feel much for her

> because I disliked her. My mother did hit me a lot when I was young, from about the ages of six to eight. I can remember standing in the kitchen waiting for dad to come home from the office. I used to watch the clock, I couldn't wait for it to reach 6.30 because he used to come home by then. And then the hitting would stop.

Eventually neighbours alerted Helen's grandparents and from the age of eight she lived with her grandmother and grandfather.

Many of the children remembered the period preceding their parents' separation as chaotic and unpredictable. Often the children's feelings of anxiety and confusion were so strong that they felt overwhelmed and helpless, as first John and then Tony relate:

> They used to argue, but it's remarkable because they had these really big rows and then the next moment they'd both start laughing and be talking and laughing together. You know it's amazing how quickly emotions can change. It just totally baffles me.

> Your mind flows if you hear your mum and dad having an argument or a fight. It stays in your head and however hard you try it won't go away, and tends to stop you from working. It disturbs you. It stays in your head.

The children found their feelings so painful and disturbing that, frequently, they blocked off and suppressed them. They remembered the general tension, and occasionally recalled a few specific incidents, but often their detailed memories of the break-up had been 'forgotten'. Pamela understood that she had done this:

> I think I blocked out most of the arguments. I don't remember very much of them. I don't remember my feelings very much. Though I do remember feeling very, very confused. I didn't know what the hell was happening, it was just all above me, and I remember feeling really helpless, and confused and lonely. Lonely was the main thing, lonely all the time. I used to feel the whole world was against me.

The children identified the break-up as occurring when one or other parent left home; and this was usually sudden and unexpected. Sometimes the break-up happened dramatically and explicitly as in Tim's family.

> It happened about six years ago. I was six and Susie was five. And I remember the fighting and the glass. The front room window was near the door and my dad smashed that and he smashed a glass into my mum's leg. We were frightened and thought someone might be hurt. Then my dad took us down to our nan's. When we went back to our home, it was night and there were two policemen outside the door and there were our pyjamas lying on the doorstep. We were frightened and a bit worried, but we went back to our nan's and she took care of us. We went back home next morning and mum said 'Your dad's gone.'

In other families, such as Sarah's the break-up was less dramatic. It occurred without explanation, leaving the children muddled and confused.

> I said to my mum, 'Where's dad?' She said, 'I don't know, he hasn't rung.' Then he came home briefly but we didn't see him, and this went on for about four nights and he used to phone up saying, 'I'm staying at a bed and breakfast, or I'm staying with my mum.' He came in one night after school and he had his bags in his hand, and he said 'Bye kids, I'm going.' 'Going where?' we asked, and he just said 'I'm going, see you later.' And he came and kissed us goodbye. And that was it, out the door, bang. I remember going upstairs and my mum's a pretty bad smoker anyway, but that night she just chain-smoked. And it suddenly dawned on me: 'He isn't coming back.'

Confusion and lack of explanation were for the children the most common features of the break-ups. The children described how they observed their parents' behaviour, as if they were searching for clues, in order to make sense of what was happening. Some children felt their parents assumed that they understood the situation. Others felt their parents believed children incapable of understanding. Either way, little was said to the child. Annie voices a common feeling:

> We kids know every single thing that's going on and can pick up even the faintest vibes or feelings, whether it's good or bad. I knew they were going to split up, it was just instinctive. I just knew it was going to happen, and then my dad moved into the spare room. And then one morning we woke up and the bags were packed, everything was gone, the bed was made, it was unlike him to make the bed, but he did. And I said, 'What's going on mum?' and she said 'I don't know.' She really didn't know what had happened, all she knew was that he got up and went. I didn't see him for weeks, and that frightened me, and I got really scared. My mum's got a double bed: and I used to go and sleep on the side that my dad slept on and cry myself to sleep for a while. No one said anything to me, I think they all assumed that I knew, and that I was bright enough to figure it out for myself. I was kind of old enough to get hurt, but not old enough to understand.

When parents did offer explanations they were often painfully abrupt and gave little opportunity for the child to explore the meaning of the changes. Both Richard and Kim described this happening.

> My mum said there was no love between them and that it was my dad's way of life, him never being there. So she didn't want to live with him anymore, that was her reason. When mum got divorced he stayed with us, for a couple of months and my mum wanted him to go, so she bought a new lock and locked him out. She left his clothes in the shed downstairs. And she told him that he had to leave because it was all over between them. So for about three months after that we never saw our dad.

> Mummy came into my bedroom and said 'Daddy and I have split up', and she started crying. She said he'd met someone else and she blamed it on him. And she said, 'You've got to be strong for me.' Then, I saw my dad, he was standing there just looking at us. That was one of the worst things, it felt horrible just to look at him.

Some parents jointly told the child of their intended separation. But this did not make it easier for parents and children to talk together. Instead the occasion took on a rather formal character with the news given as if it were a public announcement. Perhaps each parent could cope with the presence of the other only by being unusually controlled and distant. Sean and Katie were told in this way.

> They sat me in the chair and I think it was my mum who said to me first, 'Dad's got something to say to you.' I sat there and I got the vibrations straight away that there was something wrong, *really* wrong. So I sat there and my dad just came out with it straight away. 'We're getting divorced.' It sort of went in one earhole and out the other at first. I'm sitting there and then it all started sinking in and I started crying, and I think I ran upstairs.

> One day they got us together sitting in the front room, and they said that their marriage had broken down and they were splitting up. Mum actually said it, but dad said it was for the best, and neither of them loved us any the less. It was sort of as if the whole world fell apart on us, we didn't know what was going on. She said we could go and see dad any time we wanted to, but it sort of felt as if your mum's in one corner and your dad's in the other and you're in the middle.

Sharon's mother found it so difficult to tell her children about the break up of her marriage that she enlisted the help of Sharon's headmistress.

> The headmistress took us into the staffroom first and she said, 'You know your dad's not going to be coming home', or something like that. Then she took us into her office where my mum was. She said, 'Do you know what's been happening?' and I said 'No', but I had heard my mum and father in the night, but I just said, 'No'. I had a feeling that I knew what it was about, and when she said that, I started crying. My mum was crying too and she was just saying she couldn't tell us, she didn't know how to tell us.

Any explanation of the break-up usually included both parents saying that they loved, and would continue to love, the child. Although it was important for the child to hear this, many children felt such reassurances were inadequate to the situation. It was difficult to trust a parent who offered assurances of his love when he was in fact planning to move out. Pamela, who is still angry at her parents' separation four years ago, said with some contempt:

> I just think it's sort of a standard thing that a lot of parents come up with. They say 'However much your dad's and my feelings have changed, you've got to remember we both still love you.' I think that's what a lot of parents say.

The children all described feelings of distress, and shock at the ending of their parents' marriages. It was a time of unreality and chaos in which the child felt lost and helpless. Richard described the emotional confusion that he experienced.

> You've got so many emotions inside you, trying to express themselves that you don't know what to do. For a long time it built up inside me, until one day I just cried and cried. I just couldn't help it anymore. You get over-emotional. A person could be teasing you, winding you up, and all of a sudden you explode and you end up wanting to hurt the person, even though they've really done nothing much. You see, the main thing is, you don't feel it's right, you're used to having parents with you and when they split up you know it's not right.

Children felt disturbed and frightened by the conflicting demands of loyalty and love for both parents. Brian, for example, was confronted by the impossible choice of which parent to live with after the break-up.

> I remember mum saying dad was going and asking me who I wanted to stay with, but I just wanted my mum and dad to stay together. It was a big shock. I remember she said to me, 'Who do you want to live with?' and I was amazed, I didn't know what to say, I said, 'Well, why can't you and dad stay together?' And she said, 'Well, we're just not going to.' And I said, 'Well then, I'll stay with you mum.'

Faced with a similar situation, Jane expressed very clearly the profound confusion that comes when 'You don't know what to feel':

> I couldn't stop crying, I just couldn't. I didn't understand, I saw my brothers crying and I cried too. When I realised what had happened, I went to my mum and she told me about it, and I felt sorry for her. Then I went to my dad and he told me all about it, and I felt sorry for him. I didn't know who was right. I kept thinking my mum was wrong and my dad was wrong, I didn't really know. You love your mum and you love your dad, but it's ended between them. And you don't know what to feel. They're not together as parents. They're like split people, and half of you goes one way and half goes another.

CHAPTER TWO

Missing the absent parent

> You worry at first because you don't know where your father is. We didn't know where he was for six months and that's a long time, anything could have happened to him. We thought in a way he didn't want to know us any more and that was even more frightening because we thought we'd done something wrong. We didn't know what was going on.

Often when one parent leaves the family home the children have to carry a double burden of uncertainty, as Richard has expressed. They must cope not only with the parent's absence but also with not knowing where that parent is. This can fuel many fears and fantasies: that the parent no longer loves the child, that the parent is living far away, in poor conditions. Sharon describes these fears.

> When he first went I imagined him to be in a bedsittter place and I imagined the worst. I imagined it was like what you see on telly, one room and a bed, like a cell. I used to dream about it and I saw just a few chairs and a radio in one corner.

For many children, the worst of all these fears was that they would never see the absent parent again. Pamela felt that her father would immediately go beyond her reach:

> I really thought I wasn't going to see him again because the only thing I knew about divorce was that if you divorced you stayed with your mum and you never saw your dad again. I remember actually asking my dad 'Which country are you going to go to?' I really did.

For some children that fear became reality and there had been no contact with the parent for several years. In other families contact was established on a known and regular basis and that was reassuring. The children often put considerable effort into maintaining the relationships with their parents. Helen, for example, went gliding with her father, although she found it frightening, because that was what he enjoyed, and 'I wanted to be with him.' And Pamela described the effort she put into her relationship with her father, which she felt her father did little to repay.

> I think my dad's frightened to put anything into a relationship that he's not going to get anything out of. I think he probably thinks 'What can I get out of knowing a teenager?' I don't have much of a relationship with him, but I am really trying hard.

Other children felt there was little they could do either to maintain or to improve their relationships with their absent parents. Terry described, in a flat monotone but with great sadness, his father's gradual withdrawal from the family.

> We used to visit him. He used to come and collect us quite often, but then when he got married he stopped because his wife didn't want him coming to visit us. He's got two other children now. I see him about once every six months. The last time was at Christmas. And then we used to go over to his mum, our gran, and visit them and our aunt but we don't go over to that half of the family much now. We just go to my mum's half.

Broken promises, missed outings, forgotten birthdays were talked about by many of the children and these all reinforced their feeling that they had been abandoned by the absent parent. Ben was a confident and able young man of nineteen, whose father had left home seven years ago. He came close to tears as he described how his father had repeatedly forgotten his birthday. With considerable underlying anger he told of their relationship.

> I can actually count the times we've seen him in the last year. Tommy has seen him four times and I've seen him three times. I know he does shift work, but he does have quite a few days off. I'm sure he could find the time, but he doesn't. When I last saw him he came down the road and he looked at me and he didn't even recognise me. I'm more angry now than when

> he actually left because he doesn't see us much and I still haven't had a birthday present and things like that. It's like he's forgetting us now.

Some parents who left home gave their children special treats and outings, especially in the period immediately after the break-up. The children enjoyed these if they were seen as part of a continuing relationship but nonetheless viewed them with some scepticism. They had little difficulty in recognising the parent's attempts to placate their own feelings of guilt, but accepted these treats as some kind of bonus, as Annie relates:

> He was really spoiling us, taking us out to Wimpy's and giving us great big ice-creams and things like that. I don't know whether it was guilt or what, but it was pretty good at the time which was all I cared about. We had a really lovely time and he used to take us out every weekend. We got a really good education, I mean, we went everywhere in London. I know every single piece of London inside out.

When the presents were offered as a substitute for a proper relationship the children were quick to recognise the lack of real concern on the part of the parent. For Sean, it felt as if his father had attempted to 'buy him off':

> I remember once he came in a car and he had loads and loads of quite expensive toys and he brought them in and we were all excited. I can remember some of the prices were still on them. I don't know if he deliberately did that. Anyway, he brought the presents in and gave them to us and then he went and it was sort of 'That will do you.'

As children grew older and established their own interests and friends they often wanted to re-negotiate visiting arrangements. Pamela, for example, was keen to keep in contact with her father but resented spending whole weekends with him.

> My dad doesn't understand. I'm fifteen and I want to go my own way and I prefer to spend my weekends here. I say 'I get bored' and he says, 'Well, it's not my problem.' There's nothing to do over there and you know if I'm going to be bored, I'd

rather be bored here with my friends than be bored over there without my friends.

Annie's father, however, understood that she and her sister needed to have some say in when they met, as they grew older.

My dad says about my sister, 'It's her life, if she wants to stay at her mum's, that's fine and if she wants to come and stay with me, that's fine as well. It's part of her growing up, she's got to do it and I want her to have a good time while she's doing it.'

Predictably, one of the strongest feelings about the break-up and the parent's departure was anger. The child expressed anger as a way of dealing with the feelings of rejection when the parent left. This anger was provoked by and fed by the erratic behaviour and sometimes the complete disappearance of a parent. Often, the child's anger took the form of studied indifference, which Rachel and then Brian conveyed clearly:

I've got no feelings for my dad. I see him now and then when he's in London. He doesn't buy any birthday presents or Christmas presents. But it doesn't bother me any more. I've got used to it as I've grown up. I used to be embarrassed to tell other people or other children that my parents had split up. I was embarrassed, but inside me I was really upset, I could never tell anybody. It wasn't until I got older when people asked 'Well, where's your dad?' that I'd explain that he'd left home. It hasn't really affected me that much. Well I suppose it has in a way. My grandad was really my dad so to speak. I looked up to my grandad, but between me and my dad there's never really been anything much.

I haven't seen him for a long time, it doesn't really upset me. About two years ago I did see him and I went to stay with him, but I haven't seen him since, and before that I'd seen him a couple of times. I've sent him Christmas cards but he never sends me any back. I think that's very nasty. He could at least have the decency to send me a Christmas card.

Listening to the children talk about their absent fathers it was clear that often, even before the break-up, the father-child relationship had been extremely weak. Many fathers had played only a small part in family life and spent little time with their children. Often the father was described as 'never in' and 'always out working'. Sean is clear-cut about his relationship with his father, while Richard echoes his view.

> I can't really remember my father being there much anyway. He didn't take us out, it was our mum who took us out. I never really felt a part of my father, you know what I mean, the son-father relationship – all that.

> I didn't see him a lot, he used to go out very early and he'd come back about five or six. He's a self-employed builder and maybe he'd sleep for about an hour then he'd get ready and go out. He didn't have a lot of time and we never saw him.

One of the few positive aspects of divorce was that some children believed that their relationships with their fathers had actually improved after the break-up. Fathers who had been seen only occasionally before the split were now seen on a regular basis and these times were valued and enjoyed, as Mike and Richard agreed.

> When he was at home, which wasn't very often, he never used to take me out and he was very strict and always picking on me and telling me to do things. But now they've split up I get on a lot better with him and he takes me out quite often, and we have more fun. I like him better now.

> We are a lot closer to my dad now. We see more of him and we get on very well. We're thc best of friends. We see him maybe twice a week and most weekends and we keep him company. We really want to see him at the weekends. When he was at home it was just like he was there and that was it. Now it's something to look forward to. Dad's unemployed so he hasn't got much money, but we go for lots of walks. There's a little park nearby and we play football.

In general, relationships that were already close stood the best chance of surviving. Yet even these were not always sustained. A break-up introduces new stresses and changes and these must be recognised and managed if the relationship is to work. Annie, for example, was close to her father who left when she was four years old. Despite separation at this early age closeness was maintained and Annie, now a teenager, continued to enjoy her time with her father.

> I really like staying with dad, he treats me as an equal. We go out together, and go to parties and people always think I'm my dad's girlfriend and I do sometimes like, well I do it on purpose, he's standing across the room getting a drink for me and I go 'Oy, dad' and everyone looks round and it really freaks people out. We both enjoy that.

Other relationships were less easy. Years after the break-up some children, in order to reassure themselves of their importance to their parents, insisted that their parents were unhappy in their new lives apart from them. Sharon, aged fifteen, the oldest in a family of four, was adamant that her father was not happy with his new wife and stepchildren. As evidence of this she said:

> One night he came into where I was in bed and he was crying and I was pretending I was asleep, 'cos I couldn't face him. I think I'd never seen a man cry before and it might have been that, and he was saying, 'If you don't love me, I don't blame you, but I still love you. You're my daughter and nothing can change that.'

Above all the children needed to feel that they could express their thoughts freely without being censored by their parents. Yet all too often this proved impossible. Tracey's mother, for example, insisted that Tracey was happier and more relaxed since her father had left home. But Tracey herself was uncommunicative. She showed no interest in talking about the events either surrounding or after the break-up. It was only when she was asked directly whether her life was different without her father that she responded: she picked up a cushion from her bed, swung it round her head, faster and faster, and said, 'I can't cuddle him, I can't cuddle him every day.' But in some families, children were able to talk about their feelings without fear of offence or contradiction. Barry, aged eight, was partially deaf and dyslexic. He knew he would be unable to take part in an interview with his two older brothers, so he asked his mother to write down his story:

> When I was a little baby, dad left us and he moved to Laura's house and I can't see him when I want because he lives so far away. I wish my dad lived near to me so I could see him when I wanted to and when my bike goes wrong dad could help me mend it, and when my toys go wrong, he could fix them. I could pop in and see him and he could play with my toys with me. I think if dad lived with us, then one parent could rest while the other did the work, then they could change over, so mum would have lots of help with the work. Dad could take us out in the car.

Apart from their parents' divorce, the children in this family had many problems. One older brother was also partially deaf and the other dyslexic. Yet their mother encouraged the children to express themselves and did not feel threatened when they did so. Despite all their problems, the children came across as resilient young people.

One way that children found to express their feelings was to use their brothers and sisters as some sort of 'ventriloquist's dummy' to speak out the feelings of loss that they themselves denied. Nicky, for example, claimed that she did not mind at all that her mother had left home, but that her brother and sister missed her mother very much.

> It doesn't really worry me that much that she's gone away, but my sister, she's only seven, she misses our mum. I don't, seeing that I'm the eldest and I'm nine and I don't cry all the time. Peter, he's six, whenever he sees her, he talks like a little baby.

Barbie showed a similar indifference to her father's departure but described in some detail her brother's reactions:

> My little brother was really badly behaved, crying and screaming all the time. He used to get very upset when he'd seen dad and when we came home he used to cry because he wanted to see him again as soon as my dad had gone. He wanted to bring him straight back. He was saying 'It's not fair, other people see their dad all the time.'

Yet most children, and even those who subsequently expressed indifference, spoke openly of the pain they felt at the time the parent left, like Kim:

> I used to cry and I had bad dreams. I used to think, I wish daddy was here, and stuff like that because he used to sit up very late and when I woke up I used to see his light on; but now the lights are all turned off.

CHAPTER THREE

Picking up the pieces

> Your life changes when your dad's gone. We had to do a lot more round the home, and there were all the bills to pay. We all worried about what was happening. It was very confusing.

There were many changes that affected the child after the break-up: moving home, changing school, new domestic routines. But the problem talked about more than any other was money, mentioned by Mike in his summary. Less money in the family budget had very direct effects on the child: fewer clothes and presents, less frequent and often no outings and holidays. Several children were entitled to grants for school clothes and free school dinners and this often caused them acute embarrassment. Above all, money was important because it was a source of continuing conflict between the parents, as Kim and then Pamela regretted.

> I'd be in bed, and she thought I was asleep, and I'd hear mum ring my dad and say, 'I need my money right now. We have to have money for food, clothes and things like that.' They used to argue an awful lot about it and it was quite horrible. They were really nasty to one another.

> Dad doesn't give my mum the full amount of maintenance. He's really developed a mean streak, he won't pay for anything, he refuses to pay for clothes, and things like going swimming. He doesn't pay for anything he used to, and now my mum's had to take him to court for more maintenance. Mum doesn't have an awful lot of money, she worries about all the bills and her standard of living has gone down and down. And dad's seems to be going up and up, and she doesn't see the fairness of it, and I don't. You see my dad was the cause of the divorce, the main cause, and he seems to be getting all the good things out

of it. And isn't it true that men do get the good side of divorce, whereas women, they get lumbered with the kids and everything?

The most dramatic changes in domestic life occurred when the mother left home and the father took over the responsibility for the family. Children themselves in these families took on many of the household chores. Lisa, for example, described how she and her sister divided the work between them.

I think if you haven't got a mum and your dad goes out to work, you've got to help with the housework. We've got our own routine. My sister does my dad's and her ironing, and I do my own and my brother's ironing. Dad used to do all the cooking, he's a good cook, but when I was about thirteen I felt I wanted to be independent and I wanted to start cooking and he let me do bits of the roast dinner, and by the time I was fourteen I was cooking the whole dinner when I felt like it. We've been brought up mainly without our mum, and we get on just as well without her. We've all grown up pretty fast. You have to be independent.

Most children felt they took additional responsibilities for managing the home and caring for younger brothers and sisters. As a result they grew up quickly and sometimes gained in confidence. But at the same time the children resented the demands made on them and saw them as an intrusion in their lives. This was especially so when the parent did not seem to appreciate the child's efforts. Marilyn felt taken for granted.

When dad went, we used to take it in turns to do the housework, and Katie would do this room and I'd do the bedrooms or the other way round. I'd never been one for washing, but Katie did the washing and I did the ironing. And when mum came back from work she used to find the housework done, and the house clean. But after a while we stopped doing it because mum was expecting it sort of every day when she came in. And that wasn't fair. But we still look after the baby. We take it in turns to take him out and look after him.

In some families the eldest boy felt he had been cast in the role of the man of the house. Eddie, aged sixteen and his brother, Simon, aged fourteen were discussing their additional chores and responsibilities, when Simon said, '. . . and you're the man of the house now.' Eddie objected, saying, '. . . it's not really fair being called the man of the house, just because I'm the oldest. I'm meant to set an example, and I haven't got a choice in the matter.' John, who was sixteen when his parents split up, was also reluctant to take on the position of head of the household.

> When my mother found out what my father had been up to she said, in a sort of roundabout way that I would have to act as a father to the other two, and not only help them when they needed it, but also help mum as well. It was a bit ominous to start with, because, you know, you haven't had much experience of being a dad, and you don't very much like the thought of it.

The concept of 'man of the house', by definition, may exclude an older sister who has played a major part in running the home. Sharon's mother, for example, told her younger brother that he was head of the house:

> I think she told him that to make him feel better, to make him feel as though he was important, but it used to annoy me because I'm the eldest and I did most of the work.

It was not only household tasks that became the child's responsibility. Many children also felt responsible for the welfare of their parents: they talked of the pressures and problems that the custodial parent faced – management of the household, child care and often full-time paid employment. Pamela knew her mother was carrying an impossible load.

> Mum started going out to work full time and instead of her deserting the housework and looking after us, she went the other way, she became a super cleaner, she was knackered. I mean, I'm not kidding, she used to get out the hoover at three o'clock in the morning and things like that. You daren't put your cup down and whoops it was gone. I know it sounds funny, but it wasn't, it was sad.

The child wanted the parent to be strong and manage all the problems that arose. But the reality, especially in the period immediately following the break-up, was different. Life was chaotic and the parent frequently behaved in erratic ways. Some children described physical changes in their parents; John's mother lost weight, while Katie's ate too much, and became fat.

> She was very upset. She used to cry a lot. And she lost a lot of weight too, and that was quite frightening, because she'd always been rather large and then she sort of shrunk.

> Mum really did put on a lot of weight when dad went. She got so depressed and she ate and ate and ate. She wouldn't stop. 'No one's going to want me,' she said, 'so why should I care?' We didn't know what to do.

Parents were described often as tearful, depressed and lonely, and this heightened the child's own feelings of anxiety and insecurity. Rachel reacted to her mother's unhappiness in this way, but Mike was able to see some progress.

> I used to worry about her. I know she was lonely. She was very lonely. There were plenty of nights when she used to go to bed and she used to cry. I used to hear her, but I'd never go in. I was too scared to go in there. I don't know why. I used to listen by the door. I know it's wicked to say, but I used to listen by the door and ten-to-one I'd end up crying and running back to bed myself.

> She got depressed a lot, and she was crying a lot of the time, and once she threatened to kill herself. But she's gradually, very slowly got better, and now she's excellent. She used to get very lonely. She used to just sit and she didn't have anyone. She couldn't afford a baby sitter and I used to stay in most of the time with her.

Many children and their parents drew closer together at the time of the break-up and in the period that followed, and this provided support and companionship for them both. But some children were expected to take on the role of adult companion in a way that was inappropriate to their place in the family and their emotional immaturity. The child was being asked not just to grow up, but to become an adult. This was most likely to happen in families where the child was an only child. Brian, for example, was nine when his father left home five years ago, he had no brothers and sisters. He considered his mother to be his best friend, spent most of his free time with her, and described in detail their shopping expeditions and outings. To the outsider, their relationship felt claustrophobic. Brian firmly rejected the idea that his mother might remarry.

> No, I don't think my mum would want to get married again. But, you know, really I'd rather just stay as me and my mum. We're all right. You know, I'm not going to get married. I'm going to stay here and look after my mum.

Many of the other children, however, gave their parents very practical advice and encouragement to develop new interests, meet different people and begin their lives again. They did so because they recognised their parents' needs for adult companionship and because they were anxious to shift the burden of responsibility for their parents' well-being from themselves. Marilyn gave her mother practical support, while Sean tried to be encouraging.

> Dad's parting words to her were 'You're so fat, no one will ever want you, you're only good for one thing.' He more or less told her to go into prostitution, because she wouldn't be able to find anyone else, and that played on mum's mind. You can imagine, it didn't do much for her confidence. And then she met this bloke and he asked her to meet him at the pub for a drink. And we got her all ready, we did her hair, and me and my friend went down the pub with her, and Katie stayed at home and looked after the baby, and we stood there and waited and waited, and he never turned up. Mum was really disappointed. I felt like killing him. And I said to her, 'Can't you see him?' and she says, 'No.' And I said, 'Well, if you do see him, I'm going to give him such a mouthful for letting you down.' I was so upset for her that he'd let her down, because you know she really had made an effort, and she did look nice.

> I said to her the other day, 'You want to get out a bit, mum.' She said, 'I haven't got the money.' She hasn't got a lot of

> clothes, and I understand that. But I think she's got out of the habit of going out. Only last night one of the girls from the flats came down and said, 'Come on, you're coming out with me,' and this woman, she dragged my mother out, and that's another sort of milestone.

After the break-up, men with custody of children generally continued their work, and women who took care of the children often returned to work full time. One consequence of this was that the children spent more time by themselves and this was especially difficult for younger and only children. Ian was an only child aged ten. His mother had left home when he was five and he and his father lived on the eleventh floor of a tower block in South London. Ian was quiet and self-contained, apparently coping with his life, but appeared very isolated. The description he gave of his life was bleak.

> At first my dad's friend used to pick me up. And then I went to play centre at school, but now I'm ten, I've got my own key so I can come home on my own. It's much better than going places or staying at school. Then it was like school all the time. You get up, go to school, stay at school, go to bed, get up, and so on. You didn't seem to do anything else. So now I come home and if it's dark I put all the lights on and make myself at home, I watch the telly and then there's the cat and I feed the dog. I never know what time my dad's coming home because he works for himself and he's got to do a day's work and that's that. If he's late I get my own tea. Now I've got used to it on my own, it's best like that.

Tim and Susie aged ten and nine spent time by themselves each day until their mother returned from work. Tim described some of their fears.

> When there's nobody in you sort of get worried, you can hear noises. I think it's only the people downstairs going in and out, but sometimes you think someone's trying to get into our house. The other day Susie got scared and she started crying and I told her to go and get a knife. And then we went and hid behind the settee and I phoned my uncle and he came round. And he said it was just the boy next door. Mum always phones

up at half past four each day. But sometimes you do get a bit scared.

Children who spent a lot of their time alone were often very attached to their pets. Pets were talked to, cared for and played with; they were friends and companions. Ian, for example, never knew the time his father would return from work, his life would have been even more lonely without the company of his cat and his dog.

It was clear that the period after the break-up was one of considerable change in which the child had to adjust to many new routines and new responsibilities. Yet at the same time the children had to cope with their own feelings of sadness and depression at the loss of a parent. The sadness was evident as the children, like Sarah, and Lucy, talked about their feelings.

> When dad went I left the house, I went and stayed with some friends just trying to forget it. You know I'd go back home and the atmosphere would come down on you like it was real heavy. Because my mum was so depressed and because my sisters were younger than me, I felt as though I had no one to turn to within the family. If I'd had an older brother or sister that would have been a help and we could have cried on each other's shoulders. But I had no one at all to go to. And I think it's important to have someone to talk to, someone just to sit there with you and hold your hand when you're feeling really down in the dumps. I felt very insecure, incredibly insecure. And you don't seem to register anything, you just sit there and it's as though everything's crumbled around you.

> I used to stay in my room for a long time, and I didn't want to get up early for school. I don't know why really, I just was in a huff, I felt a bit sad, so I stayed in my room. I didn't like to talk to people, and when I did go to school I didn't play with anybody. I used to sit on the bench, and ever since I don't play with the children as much, but I've got this good friend and she's helped me get along better.

Perhaps the most common strategy in this period was denial coupled with withdrawal. The child cuts himself off pretending outwardly that the problems do not exist, while inwardly trying to cope with the profound loss and change. Ben became 'cut off', while Sean confessed he had behaved very badly.

> The year that he left I just kind of cut off, I don't think I showed any emotion, I just managed to keep it walled up somehow. I was asked questions but I always refused to answer them, I kept it in all the time. I used to block myself off. I was unhappy, but I didn't show it. I just kept it in.

> I was just confused. And mum said, 'You don't do anything, what do you do around the house, you're lazy.' It wasn't that I was lazy, I just didn't understand, and to tell the truth, I was bad. I smashed the house. I wrecked my room. And I can remember putting all the windows through, I mean I just lost control, I lost control of myself, I just let myself go. It was like a chain reaction, something small would start and that was it. Looking back now, I can see there was something missing. There was always something missing.

Nearly all the children said they had not wanted or did not know how to tell their friends that their parents had split up. And this made them feel even more lonely. Some boys like John and Brian (this was not true of the girls), had not told their friends even years after the event.

> I haven't told my friends what's happened, it's just I wouldn't want them to feel sympathy for me or anything like that and asking me how I was, it would just make it worse. It's not that I'm ashamed of it, I'm not, I think from a practical point of view it's the best thing that could have happened. But it's just that I'd rather go on as normal.

> They don't know my mum's divorced at school. If it crops up in conversation I try and change the subject. I just don't like talking about it. It's a silly thing, I just find it a bit embarrassing. If no one talks about it, it doesn't matter. You're the first person really. I mean, I don't mind talking to you about it. But I don't want to talk to anyone else.

Some children said they were unsure whether their parents would approve of their friends being told. They felt 'out of place' with just one parent, and feared they might be either pitied or ridiculed. Pamela and Sharon both made up excuses rather than admit the fact.

> I can remember hiding it from my friends, I used to get embarrassed to talk about it, and I didn't want them to know. I used to think that if I told people, I'd be making excuses for myself. I think I was a bit scared of people's pity, because when mum and dad were divorcing, it was scandalous then to have divorced parents. I remember my friend, her mum and dad divorced when she was about four or five, and she hid it from everyone in her class, until I started to tell people that my mum and dad were divorced. I don't think she had any good reason for it, she just did. We both felt we were the only people in the whole school with divorced parents.

> In the first year, at school, when I was ten, they used to say, 'Why haven't you got a daddy?' and I always said 'He's gone on nightwork', or something like that. And we had tickets for free dinners at school and people used to say, 'Why have you got dinner tickets?' and I was ashamed to say why, and I just said, 'Because there's four of us.' I didn't realise how many people there were who were divorced. Most of my friends know now.

School can play a vital role during divorce. The child's teacher may be the only stable adult in the child's life and can be of particular importance for younger children. Several children spoke of their teachers with warmth and described them as friendly and supportive. But for the teacher it may be difficult to judge the appropriate reaction to the child's situation. The child may mistake the teacher's concern for pity, over-indulgence or intrusive curiosity. Sarah had strong views about her teachers.

> I wanted to be understood, but I didn't want people to make concessions for me because that's the most terrible thing. I knew that if I didn't want to do my maths, which I hated I could just go and sit in the medical room and say, 'Sorry, I'm depressed,' and they'd accept it. It gave me a really apathetic attitude to everything, and I thought 'Oh, what's the point?'

> It really annoyed me them saying, 'Oh, poor Sarah, her parents have split up.' The only person that was any good was my biology teacher, and she rang up my mum and said: 'If there's anything whatsoever I can do, just let me know,' and she was perfectly normal to me about it. That was really good, because it's so easy to lose your sanity, and just to sit there and float off and get totally involved in another little world. They used to ask my sister a lot of painful questions and often she'd come home crying. When they tried to question me, all I'd say was, 'I don't know, I don't know.' I do think the school's attitude is very important, I don't think they should ask questions but they should make themselves open and friendly and look as though they can be confided in, so that the child's got someone to go to.

Children responded to school in very different ways at this time: some threw themselves into their school work and did better than previously. Others found it difficult to concentrate and their work suffered, like Jane, or some played truant.

> I hardly did any work because I was thinking about things, about when dad went. I couldn't concentrate, when I looked at something it just passed through my head. I used to have long memories about parts of my life where I'd seen my dad crying, just pictures in my mind, and I used to cry to myself when the teacher said, 'Why are you crying?' I just said: 'I've got a cold,' just to get out of it.

It helped to know that other children were in similar situations and faced the same sort of problems; but often this did not happen until the child reached secondary school, as in Rachel's case.

> I thought I was the only one in the world that didn't have a dad, but when I got to secondary school I realised there were quite a few like me and I didn't feel so bad. I saw that other people had gone through what I'd been through and I felt all right then. It was then that I began to adjust within myself to living with my mum and my sister and seeing my dad only very occasionally.

CHAPTER FOUR

Acting as go-between

> For a long time after they split up I still wanted to be with both of them because I thought it was right to have a family, a mum and dad. So I was really in favour of both of them. Then I used to get really stuck in the middle because dad said nasty things about mum, and then mum said nasty things about dad, and I'd think, Oh, what am I going to do?

Marilyn summarises, a common difficulty for the child in the middle after a break-up. In most families it was clear that custody itself was not a problem: the child continued to live with the parent who remained at home and this arrangement was later ratified by the courts. Occasionally the 'other' parent made half-hearted attempts to obtain custody, but this was not common. In only one family, of those we talked to, was there a battle through the courts. The mother had moved out with the lodger, leaving her husband, two young daughters and baby son. Both father and mother claimed custody of the children, including Lisa:

> Dad came home every day after the court case and was really shaky. He went through the courts and he honestly thought that he didn't have a leg to stand on. When dad was fighting through the courts, there was a bit of bribing going on, and the bloke my mum went off with said, 'You come with me, and I'll buy you lots of presents, I'll buy you a speed boat.' And when the court case had finished my dad came home, he walked in through the door and said, 'Well I've got you,' and we started crying. And we went to throw our arms round him, and he says to my uncle, 'Don't let them come near, because I'm so happy, if they come near me, I'm going to hug them and I'm going to crush them.' So we all had to run up to my uncle and we were piling on top of him crying, and my dad was really pleased.

> I was crying because I was so happy. I wanted to run over and give him a great big hug, and I couldn't so I gave my uncle hugs instead.

The children did not want to be forced into taking the side of one parent against the other. It was, therefore, a relief when there was no battle over custody, as Jane describes

> It's very hard you know – I love them both. I don't like taking sides. People have asked me about it at school. They say, 'Who do you love the best, your mum or your dad?' and I say: 'I can't answer it, I love them both.' Then they'll say: 'Who do you want to live with?' and I'll say, 'I don't know, because if I live with my dad, my mum will get upset, and if I live with my mum, my dad will get upset.' So it's best when you are younger that your mum just takes charge of you, and says you've got to live with her. Then you've got no choice and you can't upset anyone.

Custody may not be a common problem for children but sustaining a relationship with both parents was a major difficulty. Conflict between parents often lasted long after their separation and frequently was continued via the child. One form this took was to question the child about the other parent, sometimes to the extent that it felt like an interrogation. The children found this questioning intrusive and felt pulled apart by their sense of love and loyalty for both parents. Jane wanted to be left alone to enjoy her meetings with her father.

> When we come back from dad's, mum always wants to ask us questions. She says: 'Did we have a good time?' and we don't really want to tell her. And then later on she'll come to me and ask questions again because she thinks I can answer them and she says, 'Well what does dad think of that?' I can't really answer, I don't say anything much, and then I sort of walk out of the room.

Two sisters, Marilyn and Katie, described their father's insistent probing about their mother's life. Marilyn refused to be drawn into what she saw as a one-sided collaboration with her father and managed to contain his questioning.

> All we got from dad was: 'It's my house, you've got to tell me what's going on.' He wanted to know everything about mum's boyfriend, his name, where he worked, what he did, how old he was, has he got a car, is he this and is he that? We felt we were just in the middle again, we were a sort of go-between. He said, 'Find out what your mother is doing and come and tell,' and if we didn't we'd be in trouble. And then I turned round to dad and said, 'I'm not going to say anything about mum to you. I'm just not going to say anything.'

Katie, however, had been her father's favourite, and she felt trapped between her parents. She feared she would lose her father's affection if she withheld information from him; but, on the other hand, to give information to her father risked losing her mother's affection. Her experience illustrated dramatically the pressures that can be put on a child.

> He said that if I didn't tell him I'd be in trouble, and I sort of panicked and I just told him. In the end it was too much for me, and I broke down, because mum knew that I was telling tales, and I was sort of pushed out. I felt mum didn't want me any more. In the end I just had enough, and I overdosed and I had to go and see a psychiatrist. I won't go over and see dad any more, on my own. I don't really want to see him at all. When I went over for the first time after it happened, I was really scared that he'd sort of have a go at me, but he didn't, he just ignored me, and when I came home I was in tears. I said 'I hate bloody going and getting ignored. Why should I bother to waste my time going over there?' And I sort of got persuaded into going round and giving it another try.

Clearly, Katie's father gained nothing from these events. Instead he damaged his daughter and nearly destroyed their relationship. It is perhaps understandable that the anger and hatred felt by the parents may lead them to criticise each other through the child. Also, the parents fear that the child may 'side with' the other parent and this can lead quickly to the patterns of questioning and interrogation. Not surprisingly, the most successful relationships between parents and their children developed when each parent respected and accepted the child's love and loyalty for the other parent.

It was perhaps surprising that where contact with a parent was fairly regular but where there were long intervals between visits, the child often idealised the absent parent. The relationship developed in the child's imagination since, in reality, the child had little else to go on.This idealisation of the absent parent may feed the anger of the custodial parent who then vents his or her frustration on the child. Tony understands why his mother is so hostile, but feels he is entitled to have his own view of his father.

> She has a go at me because I am his son, and she thinks she's getting at him through me, and she says he's no good and she knows that will hurt me. I don't like it. It makes me feel like hitting something or getting back at her. We had an argument the other day about him, and I said, 'I can't remember the bad times.' And obviously when you're a kid you don't, you just want to remember the good things. She says that I think the world of him; but I think if you don't see your dad much, then you do really want to see him. If I was living with my dad I'd be looking forward to going and seeing my mum, but she just doesn't understand that.

The conflict between the parents often had consequences within the wider family with individual family members lining up behind each parent. In one extreme case, Tim's two grandmothers came to blows in front of their grandchildren.

> One night my mum was round my nan's and my grandma came, she came in through the door and she told my mum to get out. And then my nan started to have a fight, and my grandma kicked my nan in her leg. And my nan's got bad legs anyway, and they got all bruised.

In other families there was a general breakdown in relationships following the parents' separation, with the children part of it, as Richard described.

> It's difficult because everything we talk about, nan says, 'It's dad's fault,' she's always running him down. I suppose it's understandable considering she's my mum's mum, but she exaggerates and makes up stories to make dad look worse than he is. It's unfair because he's not that bad, and I say, 'It's not

> true, you've been making it up,' and I used to get into lots of arguments. And in the end I'd have the whole family having a go at me. And then they'd say, I'm growing up to be just like my father.

Many children saw less of the absent parent's relatives and some lost contact altogether. This was a further loss for the child and an additional cause of sadness. But where contact was maintained, grandparents in particular were a source of comfort and security in an unstable and confusing world. Grandmothers were described as 'always there' and that 'they kept the family together'. Sometimes grandparents were sufficiently 'neutral' to be able to explain the parents' separation and help the child to come to terms with what happened, as Rachel's did. Maintaining a close relationship with grandparents and the wider family can, therefore, be very important:

> At first my mum's mum said, 'Oh I hate your dad,' like most mums, but then she understood him and she understood how my mum felt as well. And it was she who said that they weren't able to live together any more and that they'd grown apart from each other, but that they still loved each other, and I think she did quite a good job of it. I mean if I wanted to know something, I don't think I'd ask my mum, I'd ask my nan or my granddad.

In the years after the break-up many children clung to the idea that their parents would get together again. Although eventually it was recognised that the marriages were over, the fantasy of the family surviving still persisted. Marilyn and Katie shared this view.

> I was used to the arguing. I didn't like the break fiom it. It didn't bother me, it was sort of mum and dad together. Even now, when I go and see dad and the woman he lives with, or I see mum and her boyfriend sitting here on the sofa, I look at them and I think it doesn't look right to me, it just doesn't look right.

> I think it would be better if mum lived here with us without her boyfriend and dad lived other there, and we could go over and see him without his girlfriend. Then we could all go out

> as a family and they could argue as they used to, and in the evening dad could go off to his home and mum could come back here.

It was easier to believe in the possibility of reconciliation when the parents separated rather than divorced. Some children encouraged their parents not to go through with divorce, while others, like Emma, found this too great a confusion.

> I didn't like them just separating because it doesn't sound permanent. A couple of my friends said, 'Oh your mum and dad are separated, they'll be back together soon.' I used to say to people, 'Oh no they won't get back together again', but I was thinking, separation means they're having a little separation, and they'll go back together.

Pamela felt that the actual divorce had improved her relationship with her mother:

> It all dragged on for years and I wanted her to get divorced because I thought that would make everything clear cut. And one day she turned to me and said: 'Whether or not I get divorced from your father has absolutely nothing to do with you,' and I said, 'It has something to do with me.' I remember saying, 'It really has got something to do with me.' And I think since my mum has started divorce proceedings we've got a lot closer to her and we've been able to talk about it more. And now I can say to people, 'Oh, they're getting a divorce,' and that's that.

Children often felt that a bond continued to exist between their parents after separation. This may reflect the child's irrational fantasy that the parents eventually will be reconciled but may also be based in how the parents actually behave to each other. Some parents behaved in ways that suggested they were reluctant to make the break final and even that they still loved rather than hated each other. Sean and Sharon both could see there were still bonds between their parents.

> Dad used to come back in the middle of the night kicking the door, drunk. He didn't do it a lot, but he did it often enough

> that you were always worried whether he was going to come. And my mum always used to say, 'I'm not going to let him in, I'm going to get the police,' but she never did. So in a way I think she might have been hanging on to him. I mean she could have done a lot more to get him away from the house, but she never did.
>
> Dad says he still loves mum, even though he's married to someone else now. Well, he says he loves her like a sister. And he still buys her presents for Christmas and birthday. You know last Christmas he gave her ten pounds to buy something she wanted.

In one family the husband had neglected his wife for years. She finally divorced him, only managing to get him out of the home by throwing out his clothes and changing the locks on the doors. He then sent her red roses. But, most bewildering of all for the children: 'When he had an accident, she let him stay here for a week and she looked after him. She didn't have to, but she did do it. No one knows why. It's just a total mystery to us why she did it.'

The children were confused by the ambiguity in their parents' behaviour and found it difficult to understand and deal with it. They had very reluctantly come to terms with their parents' hatred or indifference towards each other and their eventual separation; and then they had to face a situation in which their parents might possibly still love or at least need one another. The child was forced to try and understand these apparent contradictions and in that process often developed a maturity unusual in other children.

CHAPTER FIVE

Adjusting to new relationships

> I felt pretty jealous. I mean after you've had your dad to yourself for a while and then somebody else comes in and your parent shows their love for them rather than you, you get very jealous, and I got very jealous. I hated it.

Liza's words are typical of children's reactions to new partners. Many children had to cope not only with their parents' separation but also with new lovers and step-parents. This was understandably difficult: the children saw the new people as intruders who would disturb the family and steal the parents' love and attention. Feelings of dislike, hatred and jealousy were common, as Sarah and Annie freely describe.

> I remember disliking him intensely. I absolutely hero-worship my dad and I'm very close to him and I always think of Tony as an intrusion, and in a way I think I blame him for the divorce of my parents. It got to the stage when I was doing things like sticking needles into his pillow, anything sharp I found would go on to his side of the bed. It was a real vendetta. You see, whether it's a father's girlfriend, or a mother's boyfriend, they take that parent from you. I mean, the parent's not devoting their attention to you, they're turning it to somebody else.

> I used to hate my mum having boyfriends. I was really jealous. I was so nasty, I used to sit in the room and give off nasty vibes or else make really underhand comments. I frightened quite a few of them off. It's the nastiest feeling I've ever had in my life meeting mum's boyfriends. That was just true jealousy. It was a horrible feeling, it's much nastier than hate and I used

> to cry over it, it hurt my feelings so much. I felt she was abandoning me. But I think if someone had talked to me properly it would have been better, but she just treated me as a very, very awkward child. She was giving her love somewhere else and that's what got me. When I used to get really angry about her boyfriends, she used to say: 'Do you want to see me when I'm old, all on my own, just with a little granny flat in a high rise block, and a dog?' And I didn't, but I still felt the resentment and there was nothing I could do about it.

Some children felt not only emotionally threatened but also that they were pushed aside in their own homes. They felt their own space was invaded by the arrival of a new person about whom they knew nothing and cared less. Katie was frank about it.

> We didn't want him here. I wanted him to go. I kept thinking, 'It's not your home, it's everybody else's but not yours.' It doesn't seem right because we weren't consulted. And mum started letting him stay the night and then the weekends. Then he started bringing his stuff in and before we knew what he'd kicked our sofa out, our television, and our table; everything went and all his stuff moved in. That got up my nose. This is our home and he's bringing stuff in and the thing I say is this, if anything goes wrong between them mum won't have nothing. She won't even have the sofa because that's his.

Others were more ambivalent about their parent's friends. Rachel, for example, wanted her mother to be happy and welcomed her friend. But she did not want him to move in and live with the family which had become much closer since her father had left. She feared he would disrupt and weaken the bond between her mother, her sister and herself. Like many other children, the loss of one parent made Rachel anxious and resistant to the idea of further change.

> She used to go out with people for an odd drink, but that was as far as it went. Then this man came along and took her out and it got serious. I think he's really nice to her and I'm pleased for her, but, I know this may sound selfish and I've told my mum this, if she ever got married again, I'd feel resentful. I would feel that he's treading on something that's mine, that

he's sort of imposing or intruding into our little circle of just us three, my mother, my sister and me. It's a very selfish thing to say, but him coming in would be breaking into my little space around me, into my little envelope of space.

Many of the children's comments implied both recognition and fear of their parents' sexuality. This was especially disturbing for adolescents who were becoming aware of their own sexual identity. One way of dealing with this was to scorn or ridicule their parents' behaviour. For example, Annie complained, 'It was quite pathetic, she thought in an almost childish way she was big going out with her boyfriends.' Marilyn made similar comments about her father.

Since he's been with her he's terrible. He's terribly finicky about his clothes and he spends hours and hours on end in the bathroom. He thinks he's a teenager but he's forty in February. He doesn't act it, he seems to think he's a right ladies' man. He'll sit there with us and say, 'Look at all those jeans in the catalogue, I want to order a pair, what are the boys wearing today?' And we tell him and he'll say, 'Okay I'll have a pair of those.' And he looks awful in them.

The child feared not only the loss of the parents' affection but also that the new partner would unsurp the role of parent. This anxiety provided a focus for much of the child's resentment and anger. Both Annie and Sarah resisted any attempt at new authority.

There was this meal in front of me and I decided I wasn't hungry. I suppose I should have made an attempt to eat it but she said: 'Go on, eat it.' And then she came the really heavy mother with me, and then I said: 'Look, I'm not eating it, don't give me that, you're not my mum, you leave me alone.'

He said I should be in bed by seven-thirty and I said 'No, I'm not going to bed at seven-thirty.' And he'd get really annoyed and I'd just sit there and my mum would get up and walk out and we'd just be left in the room together and me absolutely defying him. He'd say, 'You've got to do this, I'm your father.' And I'd say, 'No, you're not my father.' I didn't like him trying to assert his authority over me. I just thought 'No, nobody's

> ever going to say that to me.' The only person that can say that is my father.

These men and women were seen not only as adopting roles that were not theirs, but also as influencing and changing the parent. This was especially threatening for children, like Richard, who had experienced considerable change and for whom the custodial parent was now the central focus of their lives.

> He tries to take the role of a father and we don't like that because we've got a father. He's got his own son and he tries to speak to us the way he does to him. When he's here he tells us to wipe up and if we're over his house we have to wipe up there as well. And mum's changed too, she's been really influenced by him. She used to be really nice to us, sort of soft, but then when she met him and she knew she had someone to back her, she became harder. And she doesn't want to get into an argument with him. She does what he says to make her look like she's like him, but she's not.

The difficulties were made even worse when parents did not explain their new relationships or were reluctant to face the child with the reality of the situation. Children told of girlfriends introduced as housekeepers, of finding an engagement ring and discovering an intended marriage. This made the children feel they had been deceived and that they were of little importance to the parent. Marilyn understood what was happening, however.

> We went over to his flat and she was there and he made up the story that he was sharing the rent with her because it was too expensive. They've got a great big main bedroom and they've got a small spare room and they even went to the pretence of putting all of her things in the wardrobe in the spare room. But when dad went into the big bedroom and said, this is my bedroom, there were her comb and brush on her side of the bed. So we knew and we didn't think it was nice that he was covering up. It's been two years now and they've never actually said anything. They've never sat us down and said, 'Well, look, this is the way it is.' They just sort of took it for granted that we'd accept it.

Sharon heard the news from another source which also made her feel disregarded.

> My aunt came round one day. She didn't know that we didn't know and she talked about him getting married and all the invitations had been sent out. The next time he rang up I got really annoyed because I'd just found out and I started shouting and I think he knew what it meant because he rang up again and said: 'I've got something to tell you,' and I just said, 'It's no good telling us now, it's too late.'

Parents' new relationships often led to the child acquiring step-sisters and step-brothers as well as step-parents. These were not always welcome and, even when seen only occasionally, rivalries between the families could develop in dramatic form. Lorraine and her brother Dave, for example, came into conflict with their mother's boyfriend Pete and his daughters Susie and Pam over Christmas dinner.

> It was Christmas dinner, which is a special occasion, and mum always gives us a really big dinner. She says, 'Well, if you're not hungry, leave it, but if you are hungry, it's always there.' Anyway Dave ate some and then said to mum, 'Can I leave the rest?' And she says 'Yes.' But Pete said to Dave if he didn't eat his dinner he couldn't have any pudding. Then Susie and Pam didn't eat all theirs, and they were going to be allowed to have some pudding. So I said, 'No, they haven't eaten it, they don't get no pudding either.' And Pete was absolutely shocked at what I said, but he said, 'Fair enough, they haven't eaten their dinner, so they don't get their pudding.' So no one ate their pudding. But then Pete left some of his dinner and mum says to Pete: 'Do you want some pudding?' And he says, 'Yes please.' But then I said, 'Don't give him any.' And mum was shocked. So he never had any, no one had any pudding. And mum said: 'I've been bloody working in the kitchen and no one's eating the pudding,' and Pete said, 'Well, we'll just have to have it for tea.' Then Pete starts shouting at mum and mum starts crying. I said, 'What's the matter?' and she shouted at me, so I started crying. I went upstairs to my nan and then my nan started crying, everybody was crying. It was a horrible Christmas.

Quarrels and skirmishes with step-siblings were common. But often the rivalries became less acute with time and sustained contact: the children became friends: 'We don't feel strangers to each other now.' But children had very firm ideas about who was entitled to be called a member of the family. Step-siblings might become 'sort of cousins', but were unlikely to be recognised as brothers and sisters. A child born to a father's new wife was, however, 'half theirs and half ours, so she's our sister.' It seemed important to the children that their definitions of family were accepted – perhaps in this way they felt they had some power to control the situation.

It was more complicated, and potentially more difficult, adjusting to step-siblings who came to live in the child's home. The tensions were sometimes made worse by limited accommodation – in particular, the children hated sharing their bedrooms with these new relations. Tony, aged fourteen, described the difficulties both families experienced when he, his two sisters and mother, went to live with his mother's new husband and his four children.

> I'm close to his daughter, she's a bit older than me. She comes and talks to me and I know everything about her boyfriend. And the same with me, if I've got a problem I'll go and talk to her about it. I don't think she looks on me as one of the family, as a brother, but she does look on me as a friend. But she wasn't very happy when we all came to live with them, and she said to her dad: 'You'll have to choose between me or her,' that's my mum. And my step-dad said, 'Well, right, if it's going to be like that it's going to be your step-mother and you'll have to go.' My step-dad's eldest son, he's just a bit older than me and he didn't want me to sleep in his bedroom. He said: 'I ain't sleeping in that f . . . ing bedroom with him.' I didn't want to sleep in there either, that was one of the worst things. And he used to swear at my mum, he used to say: 'We don't f . . . ing want you here you slag.' And I said: 'If you say that again, I'll hit you.' My step-dad always sides with his own kids. And my mum won't tell them off either, so she won't have to get into an argument with their dad. So it looks all the time as if she's siding with them and having a go at me. You can't really call this a family, it's just a bunch of people living together. It's not a family.

It is hardly surprising that there were difficulties in adjusting to step-relations. The children felt forced into relationships that were not of their own choosing and, almost inevitably, this created tensions. This was especially so for children who were at an age when they were beginning to establish their own independence. Richard, at the age of sixteen, very much resented his mother's assumption that he would live with her new husband and his children.

> I refused to go and live with her. She said, 'Why don't you come and live with the family?' And I said, 'Mum, how can you call it a family? Those people have nothing to do with me, I don't know them. You've married him, he's your husband, he's not my father, he's a total stranger. I hardly know the man, I don't think I want to either. I've seen points about him I don't like already. It's up to me mum.'

Richard solved his problem for himself: he took legal advice and now lives with his father.

It was even more difficult to begin to accept new people when it was unclear whether or not they were permanent. Ian, for example, regarded his father's current girlfriend with dislike and suspicion: 'She's been here longer than anyone else, but it could all break up tomorrow, or next week or in the next ten years.' Several children talked of the anxiety, the confusion and disruption of repeated break-ups. Tony's experience was typical.

> At first, when my mum's boyfriend came to live with us it was all right and then there was this funny atmosphere. We used to say, 'Can we go out dad?' We used to call him dad. And he used to say, 'I don't care.' He just used to leave us standing there. I remember the day when I came home from school and he wasn't there, he'd left, it was a totally different atmosphere. Before, it was all tense and then it was all right. Now my mum's been with Jim for two years, and she left him and I said to her, 'Are you going back?' and she said, 'I don't know.' Anyway, she went back to him, it's very confusing, it is.

Yet despite all the difficulties and problems, step-relationships could work. And it was clear that there were a number of ways in which parents and step-parents could make the situation easier.

For example, it is very important that step-parents do not set themselves up as rival mother or father figures. They need to make the child feel valued, but at the same time, avoid over-indulgence or bribery. It is helpful if parents take particular care in introducing the child to the new partner, and that the child is made to feel important rather than marginal to the relationship. Children often mentioned quite small incidents as being important to them, especially at the beginning of relationships. Annie appreciated the special attention she received, for example:

> When me and my sister used to go over to dad's girlfriend for the weekend, there wasn't a bedroom for us there. And so she used to pull out this settee and she made dad sleep on the settee and let us have the double bed. I thought that was really nice.

In some families life became better organised and more stable with the arrival of a step-parent. Nicky, whose family had lived in some chaos after her mother left home, felt better cared for since the arrival of her father's girlfriend.

> My dad's girlfriend used to come and stay at our house and then my dad was getting used to her and they said that they would live together. Now, she's been here for a year and she's got her first anniversary card. I like her being here, and since she's been here she's got us slippers, shoes and boots and clothes and lots of things. She was here for Christmas last year and it was really nice, my sack was here and the little ones were over there and she did all the decorations and the Christmas tree was there. We asked her what should we call her and she said we could either call her mum or we could call her by her name, Julie. I call her mum, the others keep on forgetting and they say Julie. Guess what her nickname is? It's Stepsy.

Children respected and welcomed step-parents who made life easier and more enjoyable for their mother or father. They took genuine pleasure in their parents' new happiness as Marilyn and Naomi described, and also felt relieved of having to carry the burden of their parents' loneliness and depression. The child felt free to take up being a child again.

> He's a good bloke and he's nice to my mum which is the main

thing, after all the hardship since my dad left. It's nice that there's someone who actually loves my mum for my mum and he treats her really good. He's a nice bloke, I mean, he doesn't come down as a father figure on top of us. He's just like my mum's friend, but really it's my mum's boyfriend and he's nice.

I think it's good because she isn't so lonely at night. Over the last two years when daddy's been away she was very, very lonely and now she's found Steve. I think it's better for her; she seems much happier. And it's much more fun, 'cos nearly every night he comes in and he plays with us and he starts teasing me. I like him being here.

Jealousy and rivalry were not experienced only by the child. The step-parent may feel threatened by the bond between parent and child, and the parent may be jealous of a relationship developing between the child and the new partner. Each person has his or her own needs which can make it difficult to give proper reassurance to the other people in the situation. Above all, children want reassurance that they will not be supplanted in the parent's affection by the step-parent. But the child also needs to be valued by the step-parent as a separate person and not merely as an adjunct of the parent. Kim, for example, warmed to her father's girlfriend, not only because she was fun, but because she treated Kim as an individual with her own views and feelings. Kim, at the age of ten, had gone a long way both in accepting the family break-up and in enjoying her new relations.

We like our dad's girlfriend. We do handstands and stuff like that and she's good fun and she's just nice to us. And she talks to us and asks us how we feel about what's happened, and I think it's probably good to get these things out in the open. And mum's got a boyfriend now. At first I didn't like him too much and I used to get annoyed because mummy was always out somewhere with him, but you know, he's really nice to us and he takes us out to lots of different places. I think mummy and daddy probably enjoyed themselves when they still loved each other, but in a different way than they do now. And I think they like it better now, 'cos I think they both enjoy themselves more. I don't really care that they're not together. They've got two other people and I think they're happier.

CHAPTER SIX

Understanding the past

> It was my dad's fault, he was going out with someone else. Well, I think so, I don't really know, no one's ever said anything. I suppose I thought that, watching all that sort of thing on television. I didn't ask, and I was never told.

What were the reasons for the break-up of the marriages? Most children, like Brian, were not given any clear reason or direct information from their parents. But the children had thought a lot about what happened, they had come to their own conclusions and gave varied, and often complex reasons. Jane, for example, was eight when her father left home, yet she had arrived at a sophisticated understanding of her mother's needs and the process of break-up.

> He wasn't here a lot and she was getting lonely. She needed someone to care for her. She had no one to talk to at night and she was getting scared. We couldn't help her, I mean we were in bed, and we couldn't talk to her as an adult so she missed out. My mum decided in her own way to fight against it and become independent. She realised that my father was practically living his own life, and so she decided that she wanted a divorce. Dad didn't realise until after it happened what had gone wrong. Then it was too late.

One common perception was that parents changed over time. Their interests and needs became different and this led to the gradual break-up of the marriage. Rachel summed up the stages of the break-up neatly.

> Basically they grew up, and they didn't love each other any more. As time went on their views and attitudes changed. And

> they changed towards each other. They just didn't get on and then my dad got interested in other women.

Sometimes children recognised that parents had little in common to start with and marriage revealed this basic incompatibility. Annie's parents, for example, were divided by social class and John's by too great a difference in personality and way of life.

> My mum and dad came from very different background; my dad was working class and my mum came from a really middle-class background. When they met they were both rebelling against it, because it was all in the sixties and the thing to do, that sort of rubbish. It just didn't work.

> I think they were different people. She loves to go out a lot and my father never liked that. Mum would complain that they didn't have a social life, because he didn't make friends easily and he didn't like going out much. They've got very different attitudes. He didn't even like her seeing her relatives, you can't just cut someone off from everybody else: no friends, no relatives.

Several children said their parents married too young with too little experience of life. They then became frustrated and bored by marriage and gradually began to lead separate lives. Rachel understood that extreme youth was one of the basic causes of her parents' break-up.

> They got married at seventeen, that's when she was pregnant with me, so they had to get married. I think they got fed up with each other. They didn't have much of a life before they married, they hadn't had many boyfriends or girlfriends, and they lived at home. So they hadn't lived much of their lives before they got married. And then afterwards they got interested in different things, and my dad went off.

The parent who left home was blamed most for the break up of the marriage: 'It was my dad's fault because he walked out', or 'She ran out in the first place and wouldn't come back, so it's really her fault.' Occasionally, the 'other woman' was blamed: 'It wasn't dad's fault, if she hadn't come into his life, we'd still have daddy.' A few children thought that they themselves were the cause of the break-up. They described their feelings of rejection and self-blame: 'I only remember that she'd left me and that she must have gone because of me. It was an awful feeling.' With time, the children felt less responsible and less guilty, but, for some, as in Pamela's case, the thought lingered that if they had behaved differently their parents would still be together.

> I remember thinking it was my fault for quite a long time. I felt totally rejected and that it was really something to do with me. I don't know how I could have thought it was my fault, I thought perhaps maybe I got in the way, maybe I was too whiny and things like that. I felt really bad.

Kim shared these thoughts for a while, but gradually altered her view.

> Sometimes it just occurred to me that it was my fault. That if I'd been good all my life, then daddy would have been good. Afterwards I realised that they wanted to get divorced and it's not because of me. So after a while I began to know that it wasn't my fault, and I didn't feel so guilty. But I did kind of feel that if I'd been good it would have been all okay.

Most children, however, put the blame on their parents, especially the parent who left home. But, as they thought through what had happened, the children recognised something of the complexity of the situation. It was quite common, even for those children who themselves felt guilty, to come to the conclusion that it was both parents who were responsible for the marriage breakdown. Pamela described this thought-process with simplicity.

> I thought it was both their faults, I was angry at both of them. I used to switch; I used to think, 'Oh, it's all my dad's fault', and then I used to think; 'Oh, it's all my mum's fault.' Then at other times I thought 'It's both their faults', and I hated them both. Now I realise it takes two to split a marriage up.

There were different views on the ways parents should behave in marriage. Children such as John believed each partner should be faithful to the other; whereas others, like Sarah, thought an affair was no reason to break a marriage. Basically, the children were asking that the parents should not behave in ways that would split the family.

> I saw it as a betrayal of the whole family. It would have been the same if mum had done that. You just can't do that. It might seem old-fashioned, but I think our view of marriage, that's me and my sister, is that when you marry you marry for better or for worse. If you want to have lots of partners, then you don't marry, I mean that's the way to be.

> He met this girl while he was still married to my mum. But I don't understand why he left at all. I mean, if he'd wanted to have an affair with that woman, then okay have an affair; but do not walk out and leave kids, because when children are in a marriage I think you owe a lot to them. I mean, I can appreciate that people change and that's why marriages do break up, because the person you married ten years ago isn't the person that's sitting next to you now. But if you're going to have children, you owe it to those kids to bring them up and then split up if you want to. Or have an affair while they're still there, as long as you protect the children from it. But I think walking out on kids has got to be one of the worst things.

Other children, however, accepted reluctantly that relations between a couple can become so bad and so destructive that both parents and children suffer. Rachel had observed this happening in another family.

> I don't think parents ought to stay together for the sake of the children. I've got a friend whose parents stayed for the children's sake and it got worse and worse; they had separate food cupboards, separate times for eating their dinner, they wouldn't speak to each other, and they had separate bedrooms. If her mum was in and her dad came in, then her mum would go out. But when it got to having separate food cupboards and one wasn't allowed to use the other's food, that was the end. It was hell and the kids did suffer.

The desire to understand the reasons for the failure of their parents' marriages deepened for some children as they grew older.

Their own experience had now broadened so that the explanation they had originally been given seemed increasingly inadequate. New questions became important which required different sorts of answers. But little was said and the child was forced again to speculate on the basis of clues and scant knowledge. Sean shared this view that children needed progressively to be told more as they got older.

> My mum used to say, 'The only thing that's wrong with your father is that he can never take responsibility and that was his problem.' That was probably her shorthand for giving me the reason why he left, that's all she ever said about him. We've never sat down and gone deep into why he left, and what actually happened between them, my mother and father. It has just been there, and everyone's gone trudging along knowing there's something missing but frightened to actually talk about it. We've never talked about our situation as people, about what has happened to our family.

Many children recognised that the break-up of the family had changed them. Annie commented: 'Divorce, it's made me a completely different person, completely different from how I'd be if they'd stayed together.' Helen felt the experience had affected her in many ways, but, in particular, it had made her more withdrawn and lacking in confidence.

> I think one of the things that's happened is that I avoid confrontations, and I don't argue, it frightens me. I think I'm afraid the relationship will end as it did with my mother. I tend just to withdraw and become very cold, but I never raise my voice, I'm frightened of losing any friendship. I think I haven't got much confidence. I find it very difficult to make friends, I always feel that people don't like me, and I've always felt obliged to entertain them. I was always the one who would do practical jokes, or poke fun at other people. I always seem to be trying to be the sort of person they would like me to be, and it's a bit of a strain sometimes. When I go round to friends' houses, occasionally the friend I want to see will be out, and then I'll spend the afternoon just talking to their mother or father, which I enjoy tremendously, and once or twice I've actually gone round to my friends knowing that they will be

> out so that I can have a conversation with their parents. And the teachers at school I got on well with, I used to sort of push them into caring for me.

It was common, as Helen described, for children to seek out adults with whom they could discuss and explore issues which they found difficult to understand. Tony on the other hand described divorce as 'weakening' the child's confidence in making social contacts.

> I think divorce makes children weaker. If your parents were together, and, say, you were getting bullied at school, you'd stand up to them. But now if someone comes up to me and wants to have a fight or starts bullying me, I'd rather get beaten up than fight back. You see, so many bad things have happened to our family I just don't want to fight or anything. I just want to get on with my life.

Many children felt that, as a protection against further hurt, they had become defensive: 'I locked myself into a little world of my own'. They were wary of new relationships. They were reluctant to trust people and slow to make friends, a failing Sarah saw in herself.

> I think it can emotionally cripple people. I know I'm very reluctant to show emotion. I have to know someone very well before I trust them. It's made me very defensive and I really stick up for what I want, I don't let people come and walk all over me. Because I think when your parents split up, even though you don't want to, you become very selfish and self-centred. I know I did, I just thought that I'm the only person that's going to get me through this.

Nevertheless, some children thought there had been personal gains. Many had taken increased responsibilities in child care and running the home, and this in turn had fostered maturity. The child had become more competent, self-reliant and confident. Sharon claimed: 'It set me up for life, that divorce experience.' And Ben confirmed this:

> Since he's left I've come out of my shell more. I was quite a shy person, I suppose I was over-shadowed by my dad. I've

had to do lots of things that I wouldn't have done if he was still here. I've grown up quickly and I'm more mature now.

Listening to the children talk, it was remarkable how much effort had been put into attempting to understand divorce. And out of this came a striking awareness of their parents' needs, and often, a generosity and tolerance towards them. Pamela expressed her understanding with care:

> I think things get easier as you get older, you become more adult, and you realise that your parents are people, and not just your parents. You realise that they want the same things out of life as everybody else, they want a steady relationship and somebody they care about. Just because they're divorced it doesn't mean to say that that's it, they can't have anyone else.

Some children also recognised that, although their parents were now divorced, they had once been happy together and divorce itself did not necessarily cancel out the positive parts of marriage, and it was reassuring for the children to know this. It helped them come to terms with the break up of the family and gave them confidence to face new relationships.

> My mum and dad were married fourteen years and then split up. But it wasn't really a waste of time. If you think about it, they loved each other a lot most of the time. It seems a waste because it's all ended, but it wasn't really. And it can't be a complete waste of time because we're all here.

CHAPTER SEVEN

Offering advice to parents

> There was no one to talk about it, no one to talk to. Parents should tell their children what is happening. No one ever talked to us, we were just left to find out for ourselves.

Nearly all the children felt very strongly what Jane had said, that parents could do much more to help them both at the time of separation and in the period that followed. Above all, they wanted their parents to explain and discuss what was happening. Children wanted to be consulted and involved in the decisions that were made. They needed to know and understand the implications of these decisions: Who was the child going to live with? Did this mean moving house and changing school? Many children stated simply, 'They should speak to us about what is going on'; and 'They should have discussed it more so we understood better'. Others, like Terry, spelt out in more detail what parents could do to help the child.

> I think parents should talk about it with the kids and see what the kids' point of view is and how they feel about it. And they should talk about how they're going to work it out and get jobs and a new house. Then the kids will be able to understand what is happening. And they should let them know that other people go through this, because we thought we were the only ones.

Sean and Annie had both hated not being told anything at the time the break-up was happening.

> Parents should bring the children into it and explain the situation. I mean, the younger ones won't understand as much as the older ones, but they should still explain to the child what's going on 'cos even the little ones understand more than they

> think. Just to walk out and leave like my dad did leaves you in a big confusion. You end up so confused, you don't really know what's going on.

> I think children should be told what's going on. It shouldn't be kept a secret from them. In my case, my dad came back to get his clothes and went off again. I think it shouldn't be like that. You want to know why he's going and when you're not told till much later it's more difficult for you to accept what's happened, because you're always questioning yourself, and asking yourself why one of them has done a thing like that.

It is important not to underestimate the confusion and pain that result from ignorance, and the burden that is placed on children who are forced to try and work out for themselves what is happening. Jane, for example, was so confused and distressed that she thought of suicide.

> Sometimes, I used to sit in my bedroom just thinking about all these things and I thought: 'Well, I haven't lived very long, I'm not very old and this is bad enough, just living these few years,' and I wondered what the rest of life was going to be like. I mean, I opened the window occasionally and looked out and thought, 'Shall I?', but then I said 'No, I don't think so.' When there's no one to talk to, you can destroy yourself.

Some parents did give basic information at the time of the break-up. But generally, there was little discussion then or later. The child needed time to adjust to the shock of the news and then wanted to talk about and explore the meaning and implications of the separation, as Marilyn explained:

> We didn't talk much, we had a sort of fifteen-minute conversation and they said, 'We're splitting up and we love you,' and that was it. But I think they should talk and explain more to the child about what's going on and about what the children feel. We had a sort of bewildered feeling. We wanted to know more of what was going on but we just had that fifteen-minute discussion. Yet it was the end of our lives as we knew it.

The desire to know and understand was striking. But at the same time it was important that children were not overwhelmed with information or told things inappropriate to their emotional maturity. Helen, for example, recalled the way her mother talked about her father's affairs when she was only seven. She understood even then that this was wrong and damaging to herself.

> She'd say that why we didn't get any holidays was because he was spending all his money on this woman. I didn't believe her. It annoyed her because she thought I preferred his company to hers. I think she was jealous and she tried to run him down. She also told me he was having an affair with the office boy which I just didn't believe. I suppose I didn't really understand what it meant, but I knew it was something pretty sordid. I really despised my mother because I could see what she was doing. I knew I shouldn't be told those sorts of things. I knew it wasn't healthy for me to hear that.

Time and time again, children talked not only of wanting more detailed explanation at the time of the break-up, but also of needing different information as they grew older. They felt that discussion and explanation should be part of a continuing process in which the parent respects and responds to the child's changing needs. Ben felt this was a definite lack for him, some years after the event.

> I know she said that he'd left, for another woman, but I can't remember my mum actually sitting down and talking to us about it. I'm sure she did but I can't remember now. I would have liked to have talked more about it, and especially when things had calmed down a bit. I wanted to know what really happened. And now I'm older I could understand more.

The children wanted not only explanation and discussion, but also the freedom to express their emotions. It was as if children needed permission from their parents to do so, yet they knew that their parents were too involved in their own feelings to take those of their children into account. Consequently, their emotions were often pushed under the surface, leaving the parent free to comment that their children were largely unaffected by the break-up. Helen and Tony contradicted this parental view.

> I think children's feelings are generally disregarded by their parents, because they're more involved with their own problems. They seem to forget that their children are there. They think if you're a kid you've got no feelings; just leave them alone and they'll get over it. You see, children aren't very good at expressing themselves if they feel distressed or angry. I wasn't. I didn't really show anything much. So parents think children aren't experiencing these things. But they are. And parents should know this.

> My mum thinks that I can't remember things, but I can. I can remember things from when I was little and how I felt, but I wouldn't dream of telling her because I just wouldn't want to upset her. But I would like to have talked to her about what I was feeling. I think it's a real mistake to shut yourself off in your own little world. I think it's bad if you start pretending the pain isn't there and you're not hurt. You should talk about how you feel with your mum and dad, and they should talk to you.

It is parents who divorce, not children. The children wanted to continue their relationships with both parents and they felt more could be done to make this possible. For example, parents who leave could show that they love and care for their children and are still involved in their lives. They could spend time with the child, not just odd days, but weekends, and holidays. They could arrange to see the children regularly and on a basis that is known and understood by the child. Above all, children felt that the custodial parent should be supportive and not put obstacles in the way of their continuing relationship with the other parent. Contact is part of being loved, as Mike and Rachel explained:

> What I really want to say is that if they're going to split up, they should both see the child, I think that's fair. If the father's going to go away he should come to see the children regularly, so that they know him, so that they can speak to him and tell him what's going on. Then he'll be interested in what they do and involved in them growing up. And then the children will feel they still know him.

> Parents should keep in contact, they should take the children

away for weekends, and see them for odd days during the week and let the children know that they still love them: let the children know just because they've split up it doesn't mean that they're not going to see them, that's what I'd stress. And show the child that you do actually love them. I didn't see my dad for a long time and I felt neglected after a while. You think: 'Doesn't he love me?' And I began to say, 'Well, he doesn't,' and I'd think; 'Well, I don't love him either.'

The children felt love and loyalty for both parents. So it was distressing and painful when they felt used, 'to get at the other', in the continuing conflict between parents. The children wanted to understand the separation but they did not want to hear one parent criticise and abuse the other. Like Tony, they did not want to be the recipients of their parents' anger and hatred.

Above all, a parent shouldn't run the other parent down. Parents shouldn't try and turn their children away from the other parent. I don't think they should have a go at the children for what their father or mother was like. I don't think she should say: 'Your father's a right bastard.'

Visits to parents were frequently marred by one parent pumping the child for information about the other. This placed children in an impossible situation: to please one parent meant being disloyal to the other parent. Often this situation continued for years. Tom and Katie, like many others, described feeling pulled apart by this conflict of loyalties. They were sad that their relationship with each parent was not recognised and respected.

I think parents shouldn't play one against the other and try to get information out of you. Whenever we came back from seeing dad, mum always asked: 'What did he say? What's his flat like?' and all those sorts of things, and we felt it wasn't right to give her answers. I think they should try and work it out because in the long run it's the children who go through it more than the parents.

It's always 'What's your mother doing?' and mum asks questions, too, and we don't like that. I don't think they should try and get information out of you about what's going on and

> play you off against the other. You see, they can get married again, they can go through their lives and have different partners. But to us we'll always have them as mum and dad. They belong to us rather than they don't belong to each other.

Children, understandably, did not want their parents to fight one another, and instead wanted them to be friends. It was easier to continue a relationship with both parents if they behaved in a friendly way; and perhaps, too, the child saw friendliness as an affirmation of what had once been good in the relationship. Barbie thought this would help acceptance of the break-up more.

> They should still be friends, even if they can't live with each other and they get divorced. It doesn't matter if they love each other or not. But they shouldn't hate each other. It will be a lot easier and better for the children if they're still friends.

Children gave other advice to parents in this situation. For example, Tom thought that once separation has been decided it should be definite and explicit. It is very bewildering for a child to have a parent move into another room or leave home and then return. Several children, like Terry, said it helped to be sent to a safe place at the time of the actual break-up – but if this occurred, the children need to understand the reasons and not feel they are being sent away.

> We used to come home from school and close the door behind us and think, Why is he sleeping in one room and my mum sleeping in another? And we didn't know what was going on. I think if they're going to do it they should do it quick so that you know what it means.

> When they're divorcing, they should tell the kids and send them off to a relative's place, a good reliable relative like a grandmother, or an aunt. Then they're somewhere stable while the parents are sorting out what's happening.

Kim and Sarah believed that constructive efforts to do something about the unhappiness caused by the break-up indirectly helped the children as much as the parent.

She didn't go out for some time, all she did was housework, clearing up and washing the dishes and she used to get very cross and she started to cry when she got upset. But now she goes out when she wants and she's not as cross and she's much nicer. I think parents should go out and enjoy themselves.

It was quite a long time before she stopped feeling depressed and started to go out. I'd recommend the society Gingerbread, which was very good for her. It helps to be with people who know what it's like. And it's made it easier for us.

Many children had an impressive degree of insight into the dynamics of their family relationships. One young man, Sean, was exceptional in understanding the extent to which families repeat ways of relating to each other, so that individual family members become trapped in these patterns of behaviour. Sean believed that it was impossible for parents to help their children to a clearer understanding without first developing a deeper understanding of themselves.

I think that before you can actually pursue your own life, you must understand your relationship to your parents and your parents' relationship to you. People live in their ignorance which isn't their fault, they get trapped in it and it's like a chain reaction. But you've got to get out of it. My family's split up and so did my mum's. But no one's ever tried to work out what's happened. What parents must do is understand themselves before they try and understand their children.

APPENDIX 1

Getting help

Legal Help

Citizens' Advice Bureaux and Legal Advice Centres and Law Centres will give advice to both children and parents. They provide information, give details of legal aid and, if necessary recommend a solicitor. Legal Advice and Law centres do not advise on the legal process of divorce but will deal with problems such as social security and housing which result from matrimonial breakdown. Addresses of local Citizens' Advice Bureaux and Law Centres are in local telephone directories.
Central offices are:

National Association of Citizens' Advice Bureaux
Myddleton House,
115–123 Pentonville Road,
London N.1.
Tel: 01-833 2181

In Scotland:

Scottish Association of Citizens' Advice Bureaux
82 Nicholson Street
Edinburgh 8
Tel: 031-667 0156

In Northern Ireland:

Northern Ireland Association of Citizens' Advice Bureaux
2 Annadale Avenue
Belfast 7
Tel: Belfast 640011

Legal Terms

Custody
Interim Custody Order
In a custody dispute a court may make an interim order about who the child is to live with until a final decision is made by the court.

Actual Custody
The parent that the child lives with has what is called actual custody of the child. This parent has the right to make day to day decisions about the child's life.

Legal Custody
A parent who has the legal custody of a child makes all the major decisions about the child's life, for example, schooling, medical treatment etc. It is usual for the court to decide that the child will live with the person who is given legal custody (i.e. 'legal custody' and 'actual custody' are combined).

Joint Custody
The court may grant custody jointly to both parents. This means that parents must consult each other on major decisions about the child's life. When this happens one of the parents will be granted 'care and control' and the child will live with this parent.

Access Order
This is a Court order which allows the child to see the 'other' parent regularly. The court may decide when and where this should happen or leave it to the parents to decide.

The Rights of Children and Parents
Parents have care and control of their children until they reach 18. When parents separate decisions must be made about custody, access and financial support of the child. It is important that parents and children discuss these arrangements together. But if there are problems children may find it helpful to talk with someone outside the family, for example a relative, social worker or teacher. This person may be able to talk to the parents about the child's feelings.

In most families, parents agree about the arrangements for the child. Their decisions are usually accepted by the court, although it can over rule them. If parents cannot agree then the court will decide. Children do not usually attend the court hearings, and it is not easy for them to put their views to the court. However, in any custody dispute, the court appoints a court welfare officer or social worker to visit the family and prepare a report. The easiest way for children to make their views known is by talking to the welfare officer and asking that their views are represented to the court. Alternatively, children can write to the parent's solicitor and ask that the letter be given to the court, or they can write direct to the court.

Custody orders are not usually made when a child is over 16, but the court will still want to know what arrangements have been made. A custody order ends when the young person reaches 18 and legally becomes an adult. If a young person marries before the age of 18 the custody order no longer applies.

When parents are unmarried and separate the mother has automatic custody of the children. It is, however, possible for the father to apply for custody and, if there is a problem with access he can apply for an access order. The court bases its decision on what is best for the child, but the mother is most likely to retain custody.

Adoptive parents have all the rights and duties of natural parents. If they separate, custody and access are decided in the same way as with natural parents.

A person who lives with, but does not marry, a child's parent has no parental rights over the child. But if the parent (with whom the child lives) marries someone else after the divorce, that person becomes the child's step-parent. The step-parent has no parental rights unless he or she legally adopts the child or is given joint custody with the natural parent. If a parent and step-parent divorce then, occasionally, a step-parent is given custody of the child. But this is only likely to happen when the step-parent has looked after the child for a number of years, as a 'child of the family', or if the court feels the natural parent is not suited to looking after the child.

Conciliation Services

These services aim to help couples going through a break-up to make their own decisions about arrangements for themselves and their children without recourse to a court battle. Some Divorce Courts offer facilities for conciliation. The local Divorce Court Welfare Office will explain court procedures and advise on the availability of conciliation services. The Divorce Court Welfare Officer can be contacted through the local Probation Office (the address is under County Court in the telephone directory).

Out of Court conciliation services are available in certain areas. Local Citizens' Advice Bureaux will give details.

The National Family Conciliation Council aims to co-ordinate the various conciliation schemes. The address is:

Romany Cottage
Crawley
Winchester
Hants
Tel: 096 27 2351

The following services are affiliated to The National Family Conciliation Council.

Location & Name of Service	Address & Telephone No.
E Berks East Berkshire FCS	Magistrates Courts Slough Berks SL1 2HJ Tel: Slough (0753) 21345
Bristol Bristol Courts FCS	Albion Chambers East Broad Street Bristol BS1 1DX Tel: Bristol (0272) 20181/3
Cambridge Cambridge FCS	2 Pike Walk Cambridge CB3 9JA Tel: Cambridge (0223) 353875
Cardiff Cardiff FCS	33 Westgate Street Cardiff Tel: Cardiff (0222) 32999

Location & Name of Service	Address & Telephone No.
N Devon	Court Alwington Bideford N Devon Tel: Horns Cross (02375) 245
S Devon	76A Fleet Street Torquay S Devon Tel: Torquay (0803) 214533
Chelmsford Mid-Essex FCS	Crown Court Probation Office New Street Chelmsford Essex CM1 1EL Tel: Chelmsford (0245) 358833
Colchester NE Essex FCS	Ryegate House 23 St Peter Street Colchester Essex CO1 1HL Tel: Colchester (0206) 68348
Coventry Coventry FCS	Trinity House 33 Trinity Street Coventry Warwicks Tel: Coventry (0203) 58915
Edinburgh Scottish (Lothian) FCS	127 Rose Street South Lane Edinburgh EH2 5BB Tel: 031 226 4507
Ipswich, Suffolk Ipswich & District FCS	49 Fircroft Road Ipswich 1PL 6AQ Tel: Ipswich (0473) 42168

Location & Name of Service	Address & Telephone No.
Kent Kent FCS	5 Brenchley Community Centre Roman Square Sittingbourne Tel: Sitt. (0795) 76949
Leeds Leeds Family Mediation Service	26 Gt George Street Leeds 1 Tel: Leeds (0532) 452986
London (Central) Div Conciliation & Advisory Service	38 Ebury Street London SW1 0LU Tel: 01 730 2422
London (South-West) Richmond Mediation in Divorce	51 Sheen Road Richmond Surrey Tel: 01 940 8066
London (South-East) SE London FCB	5 Upper Park Road Bromley Kent Tel: 01 460 4606
Middlesbrough Cleveland FCS	St Mary's Centre Corporation Road Middlesbrough Cleveland Tel: M'brough (0642) 222967
Newcastle-upon-Tyne Conciliation Service, Northumberland & Tyneside	MEA House Ellison Place Newcastle-upon-Tyne NE1 8XS Tel: Newcastle (0632) 619212
Norwich Norfolk FCS	Charing Cross Centre 17/19 St John Maddermarket Norwich Tel: Norwich (0603) 20588

Location & Name of Service	**Address & Telephone No.**
Plymouth Plymouth & District FCS	8a The Crescent Plymouth Devon PL1 3AB Tel: Plymouth (0752) 27999
Reading Berkshire FCS	1st Floor 10 Friar's Walk Friar Street Reading RG1 1LA Tel: Reading (0734) 599833
Salisbury	Probation Offices 50 Bedwin Street Salisbury Wilts SP1 3UW Tel: Salisbury (0722) 27716
Sheffield Sheffield FCS	c/o Magistrates Court Castle Street Sheffield S3 8LU
Southampton Southampton FCS	The Court House Castle Square Southampton SO1 0EE Tel: S'hampton (0703) 30996
Sunderland Sunderland & S Shields FCS	17 Hillside Sunderland SR3 1YN Tel: S'land (0783) 286598
Surrey Surrey FCS: Locations at Epsom/Staines/Guildford/ Reigate/Dorking & Esher	155 High Street Dorking Surrey Tel: Dorking (0306) 882754

Location & Name of Service	Address & Telephone No.
Swindon Swindon FCS	Court of Justice Princes Street Swindon Wilts Tel: Swindon (0793) 27285
York York Family Mediation Service	15a Clifford Street York YO1 1RG Tel: York (0904) 56727

Marriage Counselling

Marriage Guidance Councils are available in most towns. See local telephone directory or contact:

National Marriage Guidance Council
Little Church Street
Rugby CV21 3AP
Tel: 0788 73241

Location & Name of Service	Address & Telephone No.
London London Marriage Guidance Council	76A New Cavendish Street London W1M 7LB Tel: (01) 580 1087
Scotland Scottish Marriage Guidance Council	26 Frederick Street Edinburgh EH2 2JR Tel: (031) 225 5006
Northern Ireland Northern Ireland Marriage Guidance Council	76 Dublin Road Belfast BT2 7HP Tel: Belfast (0232) 223454

Location & Name of Service	Address & Telephone No.
London National Headquarters Catholic Marriage Advisory Council	15 Lansdowne Road London W11 Tel: (01) 794 5222
Scotland Catholic Marriage Advisory Council	18 Park Circus Glasgow 3 Tel: (041) 332 4914
Northern Ireland Catholic Marriage Advisory Council	4 Corry Square Newry Co Down Tel: (0693) 3577
London Jewish Marriage Council	23 Ravenshurst Avenue London NW4 Tel: (01) 203 6311

Child Guidance

Children with emotional or behavioural problems may be helped by the local Child Guidance Department. Appointments can be arranged through the family doctor or the child's teacher.

Therapeutic Support for Families

Family Service Units have 23 Branches in England. See local telephone directory or contact

Family Service Units
207 Old Marylebone Road
London NW1 5QP
Tel: (01) 402 5175

Family Welfare Association—a London only organisation. Central offices:

501–5 Kingsland Road
London E8
Tel: (01) 254 6281

After Divorce: Support Organisations

The National Council for the Divorced and Separated

41 Summit Avenue
Kingsbury
London NW9

National Step-Family Association

Maris House
Maris Lane
Trumpington
Cambridge
Tel: (0223) 841306

Gingerbread: self help organisation for one parent families

35 Wellington Street
London WC2
Tel: (01) 240 0953

In Scotland:

Gingerbread
39 Hope Street
Glasgow 3
Tel: (041) 248 6840

In Northern Ireland:

Gingerbread
171 University Street
Belfast 7
Tel: (0232) 23 1417

National Council for One Parent Families

255 Kentish Town Road
London NW5
Tel: (01) 267 1361

Scottish Council for Single Parents

13 Gayfield Square
Edinburgh EH1 3NX
Tel: (031) 556 3899

Families need fathers: a group working for equal parental rights for separated or divorced parents.

37 Carden Road
London SE15

APPENDIX 2

Suggested Further Reading

Attachment and Loss	John Bowlby Hogarth Press, Vol 1, 1969 Vol 2, 1973 Vol 3, 1980
You're Divorced, But Your Children Aren't	T R Duncan & D Duncan Prentice Hall, 1979
Beyond the Best Interest of the Child	J Goldstein, A Freud, J Solnit Collier MacMillan, 1973
Divorce and Your Children	Anne Hooper Unwin Paperbacks 1983
Must Divorce Hurt the Children	Ruth Inglis Temple Smith, 1982
The Father Figure	L McKee and M O'Brien (Eds) Tavistock, 1982
Step-Parenting How to Live with Other People's Children	Brenda Maddox Unwin Paperbacks, 1980
Child Custody and Divorce	Susan Maidment Croom Helm, 1984
When Parents Split Up	Ann Mitchell Macdonald, 1982

Families in Britain	R N Rapoport, M F Fogarty & R Rapoport (Eds) Routledge & Kegan Paul, 1982
Maternal Deprivation Reassessed	M Rutter Penguin, 1972
Divorce: The Child's Point of View	Yvette Walczak with Sheila Burns Harper & Row, 1984
Surviving The Breakup: How Children and Parents Cope With Divorce	Judith Wallerstein & Joan Berlin Kelly Grant McIntyre, 1980

AN A-Z OF CHILDREN'S EMOTIONAL PROBLEMS

Tom Crabtree

All children go through problem patches; times when they're difficult to understand, moody and miserable or when they're faced with situations with which they cannot cope. This book provides parents with exactly the practical, down-to-earth advice they need to help them through the times of emotional crisis with their children that are part-and-parcel of modern family life. This is not a book of psychiactric theorizing, but aims to do three things: to reassure parents that, whatever their child's problem, they are not alone; to give advice on what to *do* with the child and, finally, to tell them what help is available if the problem becomes too serious for the parents to cope with alone.

There are over a hundred entries arranged alphabetically, and, from shyness to exam phobia, stealing to thumb sucking, Tom Crabtree offers sensible, balanced advice for worried adults treading the tricky path of parenthood.

DIVORCE AND YOUR CHILDREN

Anne Hooper

Anne Hooper interviewed many divorced couples, and also some of their children, to find out how they coped, the difficulties they encountered, and what finally happened to them – and combines their experiences with a great deal of practical information, including names and addresses of agencies that offer divorce counselling and other forms of help.

'The book doesn't stop at the emotional effects of divorce. There's an examination of more practical problems too, such as loss of income, getting a job and housing . . . above all this is a positive book, with an emphasis on overcoming problems, as well as the potential for growth and change which a divorce responsibly handled can offer.'
Mother & Baby

'a sensitive little book'
The Times Educational Supplement

'the coverage of more complex issues such as 'telling the children,' 'sex and the single parent' and 're-constituted families' makes it a valuable book'
Marriage Guidance Journal

Also in Unwin Paperbacks

DIVORCE AND YOUR MONEY

W. M. Harper

Money is usually the biggest problem for most married couples about to divorce. What do you do about your house? Can a husband eject his wife from the family home? Can a wife lay claim to her husband's capital or inheritance? Does infidelity affect maintenance? If a wife leaves her husband, will he have to maintain her?

William Harper answers these and many other important questions and sets out advice on a wide range of problems. The author is *not* a lawyer, but has been through the divorce courts in a legal tussle that lasted over seven years. He soon realised that most people caught up in the trauma of divorce don't understand how the courts work or how the divorce will affect them financially. This book is written to help others avoid the difficulties he encountered through ignorance of the law.

'sets out in a relaxed and readable way to show all husbands and wives what their respective financial rights and obligations will be'

Good Housekeeping

'answers the questions ordinary people are likely to ask when entering the divorce stakes'

Financial Weekly

GOING SOLO

Jacqueline Dineen

This book suggests ways in which the individual can cope with the initial period of shock after separation. The breakdown of a personal relationship, whether a marriage or a long-term living together, is so common that outsiders tend to take it for granted. For the people involved, the emotional trauma is as severe as ever it was. This book aims to help the person involved in such a break organise their life into some sort of order, able to cope with day to day life and new relationships. The practical problems of separation and divorce – money, a home and a working life are covered in detail with guidance to further sources of advice. But the main purpose of GOING SOLO is to help with the emotional problems – coping with loneliness; feelings of guilt; inadequacy and failure; building up a new social life; dealing with outside opinion; holidays; new interests and re-discovering individuality, before embarking on another long-term relationship.

STEP-PARENTING

How to Live with Other Peoples Children

Brenda Maddox

An epidemic of divorce is sweeping through all the countries of the world that observe Western marriage customs. Many more people are attempting the difficult task of replacing a parent. But for every happy step-relationship there are dozens dogged by bewilderment, resentment, guilt and even downright dislike, often not of the step-parent's making.

What are your rights and duties? How can you reassure the troubled children of a broken marriage, or win the affection of a hostile child? Brenda Maddox deals with these and many other questions. She also discusses the myths and facts of the subject and vividly describes her own experience as a step-parent.

'Covers the whole gamut of step-problems in an entertaining and informative way'

Sunday Times

'The general effect of her compassionate and interesting book is helpful and comforting'

She